The Two-Ton Secret

GAIL JARROW lives in Ithaca, New York, with her husband, three children, and a rabbit named Leo the Lop. For several years she was a math and science teacher, but now her work is devoted to writing.

The Two-Ton Secret

Gail Jarrow

AN AVON CAMELOT BOOK

THE TWO-TON SECRET is an original publication of Avon Books. This work has never before appeared in book form.

AVON BOOKS
A division of
The Hearst Corporation
105 Madison Avenue
New York, New York 10016

First Avon Camelot Printing: December 1989

CAMELOT TRADEMARK REG. U.S. PAT. OFF. AND IN OTHER COUNTRIES, MARCA REGISTRADA, HECHO EN U.S.A.

Printed in the U.S.A.

OPM 10 9 8 7 6 5 4 3 2 1

For Kyle and his dad

Chapter 1

"What are you doing?"

Startled by the voice behind him, Seth tripped over the screens, sending them clattering onto the cement.

The girl on the sidewalk chuckled as she shifted her sack of newspapers to her other shoulder.

"You shouldn't sneak up on a person like that, Phoebe," he said, bending to gather the screens scattered across the sidewalk.

"And you shouldn't be so noisy this early on a Saturday morning." She handed him a screen.

"How was camp?" He lowered his voice to library volume.

"Not as much fun as last year. I don't like being away all summer anymore."

"You look different. How come you cut off your ponytail?" he asked, immediately regretting the way the words came out.

"Thanks a lot."

"No, I mean—"

"Forget it," she said coolly. "Why are you poking into everybody's trash?"

Seth dropped the last screen onto the pile on the curb. "Go deliver your papers."

He expected her to punch him in the arm the way she used to when he told her to evaporate. But she didn't. Instead, she pushed aside a twisted tricycle frame and plopped down in the faded upholstered chair next to the screens. "They put the seventh-grade lockers way in the basement this year," she said. "It's like going down into a dungeon."

"So that's why I haven't seen you around."

"I got The Hag for english. She's already bugging me about the way I write my *r*'s. Remember, like she did you last year."

"That woman won't be happy until the entire world makes *r*'s with two peaks and a valley," said Seth.

"Even so, I don't think junior high is as bad as Hilary and the twins told us." Her tanned legs dangled over the arm of the chair. Seth tried not to look at them.

"It's only been three days," he said. "Give it time."

"You going out for anything?" she asked. "Besides basketball, of course."

"They asked me if I'd do some artwork for the newspaper."

"So, are you going to?"

"Probably." He made a face at her. "Any more questions, Madame Inquisitor?"

Phoebe swung her legs down. "I saw a lot of stuff along my paper route this morning."

"You never give up, do you?" He couldn't help smiling. "I already checked out everything between

2

my house and here. Nobody's putting out anything good this year—at least not around here."

"Just tell me what you want and maybe I—"

"I have to go." He picked up his bike. "I think I'll try the other side of Main Street. Better neighborhood."

"Why are you trying to get rid of me?"

"Nothing new about that."

"You know what I mean." The tone of her voice made him turn around.

She pushed herself out of the chair and walked over to him. "I heard about your father's job."

"Word gets around."

"They say your mom's doing daycare. It must be a zoo at your house."

"Complete with wild beasts and smelly cages," he grumbled. "That's why I'm out here."

"Toy hunting?" she asked.

"You must be kidding. The Five Little Monsters can play with the electric sockets as far as I'm concerned," he said. "I can't even use the dining room table for drawing anymore. It's always covered with Pampers and Diaparene."

"So you're looking for something to make into a drawing table for your room."

"Now you know. Are you satisfied?" He climbed on his bike and started down the sidewalk.

"There, you see? I *can* help." She hoisted her sack and ran after him. "I'll show you."

"Just tell me where it is," Seth called over his shoulder.

3

"You'll need help moving it. I'll finish my route and then we'll go to my house for my wagon."

He slowed down. "It better be good, Phoebe."

"It's exactly what you need," she said, jogging beside his bike.

"Then hurry up. I want to get there before the scavenger trucks."

"The what?"

"Those flea market guys who cruise around looking for good stuff when the town has these large item pickup days."

"No problem. I'm almost done with my route."

Seth watched as she pulled a folded newspaper from her sack and sent it flying onto the porch of a white stucco house. Phoebe had changed over the summer, but she still could throw. "You've got a pretty decent arm," he said.

"I'm a little off since camp. I need another week to get back my accuracy. I can usually land it right on the mat without hitting the door."

They headed along Fourth Avenue, Seth pedaling slowly and Phoebe stopping to toss her papers, then sprinting to catch up with him. Seth scanned the piles of junk along the curb, just in case Phoebe's idea of a perfect table wasn't. But all he saw were broken lawn chairs, stained mattresses, and old tires.

The maple trees showed a tinge of red. The first Saturday after Labor Day was early for that, he thought. Maybe they were in for a long winter. His parents wouldn't like that. They complained about heating bills even when his dad was working. This year would be worse.

4

"I could use some extra money, now that lawn mowing's almost over," he said, while they waited at the Oak Street intersection. "Are they hiring any carriers?"

"I don't think so. But kids always quit when the weather gets lousy. I'll let you know if I hear of anything." She reached deep into her bag as they crossed the street. "Only three more to go."

A few minutes later they arrived at her house. Phoebe slipped the empty sack off her shoulder and laid it on the porch. "The wagon's in here," she said, pushing up the garage door. "Better leave your bike. It'll take both of us to get it to your house."

"I only need a card table, not something made for a banquet hall."

"This is much better than a dumb card table." Phoebe's eyes sparkled as she gave him the handle of the red wagon. "Let's see you keep up with *me* this time." She broke into a run down Fourth Avenue.

Seth tried to catch her, but the old wagon slowed him. The wheels rattled as they bumped over the cracks in the concrete sidewalk. He lost sight of her as she turned the corner at Chestnut Street.

When he finally caught up, she had stopped to talk to a fragile, white-haired woman pushing a baby carriage.

"You know my great-aunt," Phoebe said. A miniature black poodle stuck its head out from under the pink blanket in the carriage and yapped. "*And* Babette."

Seth remembered that Phoebe's aunt was unusual,

5

certainly not like any of his relatives. But pushing around a dressed-up dog in a baby carriage was something new. "Hello, Miss Nichol." He smiled at her and patted the dog's head. Babette barked and nipped his fingers. Seth yanked his hand away.

"Babette, don't be rude," Miss Nichol said firmly.

"Auntie, you remember Seth Findeison from when we lived over on Beech Street."

"Why, of course. Excuse me, Seth, for not recognizing you right away. You've shot up taller than a pole bean stalk!" Stepping toward him, she looked him up and down. "And your hair is darker. It used to be almost white, as I recall. You must be nearly twelve by now."

"I turned thirteen in March," he said.

"My lands! The last time I saw you, you and Phoebe were in that fancy tree house dropping water balloons on your sister and the twins while they sunbathed."

"That was centuries ago," Phoebe said.

"They deserved every drop." Seth rubbed his tender fingers on the leg of his jeans.

Miss Nichol laughed. "Yes, as I recall, they did. Really picked on you two, didn't they?"

"We've got to be going." Seth nudged Phoebe with his elbow.

"And so do we, don't we, Babette?" Miss Nichol patted the dog's curly head. "We're a bit behind schedule this morning already."

Phoebe bent down and kissed the elderly woman on her cheek. "You need some help around your house, don't you, Auntie? Seth's a hard worker."

6

Miss Nichol smiled, and the wrinkles at the corners of her eyes stretched into her snow-white hair. "Indeed I do. Nothing strenuous, I assure you. But it does require more muscle than I, or even Phoebe, can muster. Are you available, Seth?"

"I guess so."

Immediately, Babette jumped to her feet, yapping her disapproval. Miss Nichol lifted the dog from the carriage and kissed her nose, as Phoebe and Seth waved goodbye.

"You shouldn't have asked her to give me a job," Seth said, as they hurried down Chestnut Street.

"Why not? You said you wanted something to replace lawn mowing. And she needs someone to help her out."

"I do need the money." He looked at the teeth marks on his fingers. "But I could do without Fang."

"Don't mind Babette. She thinks she's Auntie's baby. I guess in some ways she is."

As they approached the intersection of Chestnut and Sixth Avenue, Phoebe pointed to an imposing Victorian house on the opposite corner. "Here we are."

Seth gazed at the spiked iron fence surrounding the front yard. It looked like an army of black skeletons. The dark windows, framed by black shutters, stared unblinking from under the angular gables. High above the street, the widow's walk was perched on the roof like a crown. "You didn't say it was the Prescott house."

"Come on. You don't believe all the stories about her, do you?" said Phoebe.

7

"I'm not sure I want to take something from her trash."

"What difference does it make? If she cared about it, she wouldn't be throwing it away."

Seth followed Phoebe around to the driveway at the Sixth Avenue side of the property. Next to the curb sat a large pile of boxes and furniture. A silver Mercedes-Benz was parked in the driveway. It shined as if someone had spent three hours waxing and buffing it. Behind the car stood a barn, now used as a garage. The doors were open, but the interior was so dark Seth could see only a few feet inside.

"Can you believe she has so much money she throws out all this good stuff? Look at this chair," said Phoebe, as she circled the collection on the curb.

"Maybe she got tired of the color," Seth replied. "Well, you dragged me here. Where is it?"

Phoebe reached for the corner of a red-flowered drapery and pulled, dramatically spreading her arms as she did. "Voilà!"

"A rolltop desk," said Seth, running his fingers along the reddish-brown wood. He carefully rolled back the lid. "A little beat up, but I could sand it down and refinish it. Not bad, Phoebe."

"Not bad? It's fantastic!" Phoebe exclaimed, as she peered over his shoulder. "Look at all those neat little compartments. You could put your pens in that drawer and nibs in that one and ink in that one." She jabbed him in the waist with her finger. "Now, Seth Findeison, aren't you glad you ran into me this morning? Isn't this the most stupendous, absolutely perfect, unbelievably wonderful desk in the entire world? And *you* would have settled for a card table.''

''Slightly overstated,'' Seth murmured, although it *was* a prize. ''But why would she throw it out? It's probably an antique.''

''She's rich. She can do things like that.''

At that moment, a flutter of white in one of the windows caught his eye. ''Did you see that?'' Seth whispered, pointing to the house.

''Where?''

''A woman's face at the bay window.''

Phoebe glanced at the house. ''I don't see anyone.''

''She's gone now, but I'm sure I saw someone watching us.''

''Must have been Old Lady Prescott putting a hex on us,'' teased Phoebe.

''Maybe we should ask before we take it.''

''Look,'' Phoebe said impatiently, ''if you don't take it, those scavenger trucks will. Stop worrying.''

Seth hesitated for a moment. ''You're probably right.'' He pulled the wagon closer. ''Let's figure out how to get it out of here.''

The desk was awkward to move, but after several false starts and one pinched finger, they managed to wrap the drapery around it for protection and lay it on its side in the wagon.

''We have to turn around,'' Seth said, realizing they had forgotten to aim the wagon the right way. ''You steer and I'll hold onto the desk. Careful of the Mercedes.''

Walking several feet up the Prescott driveway,

9

Phoebe gradually turned the wagon in the direction of Seth's house. But progress was halted when the front wheels struck the seam between the driveway and the sidewalk where a section of crumbling concrete jutted upward.

"I can't get the wagon over the crack. The desk weighs too much," Phoebe said, tugging on the handle.

"I'll push." Seth moved his hands from the desk to the rear of the wagon. "On three. One, two, three."

The wheels jumped the crack, and the wagon lunged forward. Suddenly, the two friends were startled by the screech of tires at the intersection. A white compact car whizzed around the corner, narrowly missing the stop sign, and sped in their direction.

In the split second that their attention was diverted, the wagon coasted back over the crack. Before they could react, the wagon, with its heavy cargo, slid into the side of the glistening silver Mercedes.

The white compact skidded to a halt at the end of the Prescott driveway. An unshaven man reached across the passenger seat and rolled down the window. "Hey Findeison! Your daddy sink so low that he sent his kid to steal from garbage cans?"

Seth picked up a small chunk of concrete near his feet. As he brought back his arm to hurl it, Phoebe grabbed his wrist. "Don't, Seth!" she cried.

With a roar from the engine, the white car pulled away.

Angrily, Seth flung the concrete to the ground.

"My father used to work with that guy at the mill. If he'd heard him say those things . . ."

"Forget about him," said Phoebe. "Is the Mercedes okay?"

Seth knelt by the front right side of the car. He moaned. A deep, four-inch scratch near the fender marred the perfect finish. "One of the desk legs must have done it."

"Maybe they won't notice," Phoebe said nervously. "Let's get out of here."

But before they could move, a tall, heavyset man appeared in the open doorway of the barn. With his full beard and coal black eyes, he reminded Seth of a bear. "What are you kids doing?" he called to them.

"Uh-oh!" exclaimed Phoebe. "It's Owen Weber, Mrs. Prescott's nephew." Quickly, they dragged the wagon away from the Mercedes.

"What's going on?" Growling like an enraged grizzly, Weber stalked down the driveway.

Chapter 2

Weber stopped at the car and peered through the windshield. Then he slowly circled the vehicle, inspecting the doors and trunk lock.

Seth couldn't take his eyes off Weber's bulging biceps. He knew he should admit to scratching the car, but the man's menacing appearance scared him. He had a bad feeling about Weber—a *very* bad feeling.

Moving closer to Phoebe, he whispered, "If we have to, run and forget about the wagon."

She nodded agreement.

Glaring at them, the brawny man approached. "Where are you taking this?" Weber demanded, as he lifted the drapery.

Relieved that the man hadn't noticed the scratch, Seth felt some confidence return. "You don't want it anymore, do you?"

"That doesn't answer my question."

"He needs a desk for his homework, sir," Phoebe said.

"He does, does he?" snarled Weber. "Well, take it and get out of here. And don't let me ever catch you near my car again."

Seth's heart still pounded after they were well out of sight of the Prescott house.

"Whew," sighed Phoebe, when they stopped to cross Main Street. "My skin's still crawling. Weber is like a mutant out of a horror movie."

Seth glanced over his shoulder. "I just hope he doesn't see the scratch."

Bryan and the other guys were waiting for him Monday afternoon under the basketball hoop in the junior high school parking lot.

"You're late again, Findeison," said Jon. "Coach won't go for that, no matter how good you shoot."

Ignoring him, Seth dropped his jacket and books on the ground.

"Where were you?" Bryan tossed him the ball.

Seth caught it and dribbled toward the basket. As he shot, Jon jumped to block. The ball hit the rim and bounced away. "I thought we were going to meet in the gym," said Seth.

"Get with the program, Findeison," said Lee, bringing the ball back in and making a perfect shot, "or you won't get *in* the program."

"Forget it," said Bryan, as he retrieved the ball. "Let's get to work."

The four practiced layups and free throws, then played a game—Seth and Bryan against Lee and Jon. Although Seth had grown a couple inches over the summer and had a longer reach than the other three, he couldn't sink his shots.

"What's wrong? Your game's off from last spring,"

said Bryan. "You'll never make the team shooting like that."

"Yeah, I know." Seth wiped the sweat from his face with the hem of his shirt. He knew his concentration was off, and he knew why.

"Who cares?" Lee said, as he dribbled around Seth. "It'll improve the odds for the rest of us."

"Nice team spirit." Seth reached for the ball and broke Lee's rhythm. "But then you always were out for yourself anyway."

"Don't give me that one-for-all-all-for-one crap," said Lee, tucking the ball under his arm. "You want to make the team as much as I do. And we all know only two of us are going to come up winners. I say you'll be a loser."

"What makes you so sure?"

"I'll tell you." Lee draped his arm over Seth's shoulder. "Being a loser runs in your family."

"Shut up, Morgan!" Seth shoved him away.

"You hit a raw nerve, Lee." Jon laughed.

Bryan stepped between them. "He's just kidding around, Seth. Let it go."

"Who's kidding?" sneered Lee. "Being on welfare's no joke, is it, Findeison?"

"We're not on welfare."

"Touchy, isn't he?" Lee said to Jon. They both laughed.

Seth couldn't hold in his anger any longer. He lunged at Lee, striking his jaw with a quick, strong thrust. Stunned, Lee dropped the basketball. Then, regaining his footing, he whacked Seth in the face

15

under the left eye. As Seth fell backward onto the macadam, Lee pounced on him.

"Cut it out!" Bryan yelled, while Jon pulled Lee off. Jumping to his feet, Seth rammed his fist into Lee's unprotected stomach. Bryan grabbed Seth's shoulders and dragged him away.

Breathing hard, Seth glared at Lee and Jon. "We don't need these guys, Bry. Let's go practice by ourselves."

"I don't know," said Bryan, glancing at the other two. "I think maybe I'll hang around here awhile."

"Suit yourself." Seth picked up his books and jacket.

"You'll feel better when you cool off," Bryan said. "Catch you later, okay?"

Without replying, Seth jogged across the parking lot. Instead of turning at Beech Street and heading home, he went west on Lewis Road toward the business district. He felt like a long walk—alone.

His cheek throbbed. Yet knowing he had hurt Lee made him feel better. He was glad he finally had an excuse to pound the guy. But he didn't feel as good about what happened with Bryan.

As he passed Genuardi's, he heard someone call his name. A man several feet away lifted his grocery bag from a cart and walked toward Seth. "Don't tell me you didn't recognize your old coach."

"Max! I didn't see you there." But Seth wouldn't have known him anyway. He remembered his elementary school gym teacher as tall and athletic. This man was a couple of inches shorter than Seth and had a well-developed paunch. What remained of his hair was gray. Seth was glad to see him. "I thought—well, I heard somewhere—that you moved to Ohio."

"It didn't work out living with my cousin, so I came back. I hoped after two or three years maybe people would forget about me and my problems with the school board."

"I never forgot about you," said Seth. "I mean . . . about how you helped me."

"And I was right about you, too." Max patted Seth's back. "I told you you'd grow. Bet those layups are a breeze for you now. All that jumping practice I made you do was worth it, wasn't it?"

"I did okay last season."

"Don't try to fool me. I got the newspaper sent to me in Ohio. I followed my boys. You were an ace. Going out for varsity?"

"Yeah, but they're only taking two eighth-graders."

"I always said you had the makings of a great finesse player. My money's on you." He pointed to Seth's cheek. "Anybody I know?"

"Lee Morgan, as a matter of fact."

Max raised his eyebrows. "How about that."

"The guy turned into a jerk."

"Between you and me and the backboard, it hasn't been a recent transformation," he said. "He was never in my top twenty."

As Max leaned closer to examine the reddened cheek, Seth smelled alcohol on his breath. Maybe the rumors had been true, after all, he thought.

"I saw your sister waitressing in The Spot the other

17

morning," Max continued. "She sure grew up pretty."

"She thinks so, too." Seth rolled his eyes.

"Looks like the ice cream's melting," Max said, peering into his grocery bag. "Want a ride home?"

"Uh, no thanks. I have some things to do."

"Be sure to get ice on that face," Max said, clicking his tongue. "Take it easy."

Seth watched as the man crossed the parking lot and squeezed into his subcompact. Wrong kind of car. He belonged in a station wagon full of pint-sized basketball players driving to a Saturday game.

It just wasn't right.

"Dinner will be late tonight," his mother said when he came in. "Sit still while I tie your shoe, Jenna." The two-year-old on her lap squirmed and twisted like a worm on a hook. "Get yourself a snack. Jenna's mother won't be coming until 6:30. What'd you do to your face?"

"Walked into a door," muttered Seth.

"That mine!" The Screamer jumped off Mrs. Findeison's lap and bolted across the room.

"Oh no!" his mother cried. "Jeremy! Take that crayon out of your mouth."

Seth stepped over the Human Wrecking Ball, who was ramming his toy truck into the legs of the coffee table, and went into the kitchen. He opened the refrigerator and surveyed the shelves. Pushing aside the baby bottles, he grabbed a carton of milk and an orange. Nothing else looked appealing, so he checked the cupboard. Except for a single Oreo, the shelves

18

were filled with boxes of zwieback and Hilary's melba toast. He took the Oreo and some zwieback—the Sneak liked them so maybe they weren't too bad—and waded through the sea of bristle blocks toward the stairs.

"Don't drop that milk carton," his mother warned. She tucked a newspaper under his arm. "Take this up to your father. And don't make crumbs."

Seth glanced at the coloring books, toys, and wadded-up tissues on the floor. He wondered how a woman who tolerated a downstairs that looked like a demolition derby could be so concerned about a few crumbs upstairs.

His father, still in pajamas, sat on his bed watching television. Seth dropped the newspaper in his lap.

"You found another Oreo." He plucked it from Seth's hand.

"Wait. It's the last—"

But the man had already popped the cookie in his mouth. "Let's see what they say about the Phillies game last night," he said, pulling out the sports section.

A moose and his flying squirrel friend cavorted on the TV screen. "Dad, why are you watching *The Bullwinkle Show?*"

"Only thing on." Mr. Findeison paged through the newspaper. "When's dinner?"

"Mom says it'll be late tonight."

"There weren't any more cookies, were there?"

Shaking his head, Seth escaped into the hall. He couldn't stand seeing his father like that. He wished he could change what he'd done—untell the lie that made his father end up that way.

He tried to push the thought from his mind, but it wouldn't leave. It never left. The best Seth could do was to cover it with other thoughts and hope the memory wouldn't bother him for a while.

It was like stuffing his sweaty gym clothes in the back of his locker behind the books. Sooner or later, the smell got so bad, he had to drag them home to get washed. Only with this, there was no getting rid of the smell.

After a stop in the bathroom to examine his cheek and clean off his skinned elbow, Seth went to his room. Closing the door, he put his snack on the nightstand and collapsed on the bed.

A moment later he realized he wasn't alone. "You're not allowed upstairs!" he barked at the two small forms crouched between the side of his bed and the window.

The girl and boy stared up at him. The Whiner's lip quivered. "I had to go peepee," she said.

"Don't give me that," replied Seth. "You wear diapers."

"Not anymore." She lifted her dress. "I have Barbie panties now."

Seth turned to the redheaded boy. "What's your excuse?"

"I watch her."

Seth hopped off his bed and opened the door. "You two stay out of here." He narrowed his eyes. "Or I'll take your blankie."

Clutching her pink blanket, the Whiner ran from

20

the room crying, "Sethie mean to me! Sethie mean to me!"

The little boy followed, pausing at the door to aim his foot at Seth's leg. Seth jumped back, out of range. "I'm on to you, Shin-kicker."

The toddler stuck out his tongue and dashed out. Seth shut the door and locked it.

After his snack—the zwieback wasn't bad, but an Oreo would have been better—he moved the folding chair from the other side of the room and sat down at his new desk. He hadn't had a chance to try it out yet. Right after he and Phoebe had lugged it upstairs and cleaned off the dust, his aunt and uncle from New Jersey had shown up for an unexpected weekend visit, and Seth had had to move out of his room.

Part of him couldn't wait to lay a piece of drawing paper on the mahogany surface. Yet another part was hesitant, afraid that his pen wouldn't move across the paper the way he wanted it to.

He stared at the horizontal slats of wood on the closed rolltop. Engraved on the lowest one were the letters "C.D.P." Seth wondered if these were Mrs. Prescott's initials.

Reaching into the cardboard box at his feet, he pulled out a sheet of white paper and a pencil. He glanced at the pen-and-ink drawings on the wall. Animals, landscapes, faces. It had been months since he'd done anything that good.

He took a deep breath, then slid up the desk top.

He drew clouds, not white and puffy, but dark and threatening. The naked branches of the trees bent to one side, as if blown by a powerful wind. In the left

21

foreground stood a tall house with a steep, peaked roof and many gables.

When he finished, Seth realized he had drawn the Prescott house, though he hadn't meant to. Sometimes he didn't know where the images came from or why he drew them. They seemed to flow through his hand onto the paper.

He wasn't satisfied with the drawing. Taking his eraser, he reworked the trees and roof. But it still didn't please his eye. Why couldn't he get it right? Frustrated, he closed the desk.

The phone was ringing in the hallway. At the sixth ring, Seth went to answer it.

"Is Hilary home?" It was her boss at The Spot. He knew the voice.

"I'll see," replied Seth, even though he figured his sister would have answered it by now if she were within two hundred feet of the phone. He knocked on her door and was surprised when she responded. "It's The Spot," he said.

Hilary opened her door and scowled at him. "They probably want me to work breakfast shift again tomorrow, and I want to stay out late tonight."

"Can't lose your beauty sleep," said Seth, heading for his room.

"Just tell them I'm not home."

"He could hear me talking to you."

"Oh great."

"Next time I won't bother," he said, as she brushed past.

Later that evening after a spaghetti dinner—which Seth ate alone because Mr. Findeison took his plate

22

upstairs to watch the baseball game, because Hilary left early on her date, and because Mrs. Findeison nibbled hers while she vacuumed the living room—Seth removed his drawing from the rolltop desk. It bothered him that the image wasn't quite right, and he couldn't fix it. Disgusted, he crumpled up the paper and shot it toward the miniature basketball hoop attached to his wastebasket.

He missed.

Switching off the light, he crawled into bed. Mr. Gottshall, who lived in the other half of their duplex, had his radio turned up loud. Top of the seventh, the Phillies were losing four to two. Seth could hear the same commentary from the television in his parents' room.

That was the trouble with going to bed too early. You heard everything—sometimes more than you wanted.

It had been the first hot night of summer, and Seth had set up the small table fan next to his bed. But they were yelling, so he heard every word anyway.

"The company was looking for an excuse, and you gave it to them," his mother had said. "With all those layoffs, you should have done anything they asked. They might have transferred you to underwear the way they did some of the others."

"Who'd have thought they'd fire me after twenty years?" his father said.

"And that union you worked so hard for . . . a lot of good it did you. I bet they don't have unions down

South, do they? I heard that's why they moved the pajama division there."

"That's only a rumor," he said.

"You could have stayed. You had a chance." She started crying. "What will we do?"

"Don't worry. I already have a few leads. I'll find a new job—a better one—by the end of the week."

But he didn't. Not at the end of the week or at the end of the month or at the end of the summer. After a while he'd given up and stopped bothering to get dressed in the morning.

Seth had wanted to tell his father then. About the phone call from the mill. About the extra shift. That he hadn't enjoyed the basketball game anyway. But he hadn't been able to do it.

And now it was too late.

The ringing phone woke him. Dim morning light filtered around the edges of the window shade. Seth heard muffled voices, then footsteps approaching his room at the end of the hall.

His door flew open and the ceiling light went on. Squinting and rubbing his eyes, Seth sat up. His mother, tears streaming down her face, stood over him.

"Get up! There's been an accident."

Chapter 3

When the Findeisons arrived at the emergency room, the doctors were already working on Hilary. Seth caught a glimpse of her on a stretcher when his parents went behind the drapes into the examination area. She looked as if someone had thrown a bucket of red paint in her face.

"Is she going to be okay?" he asked his parents when they returned to the waiting room.

"She has a broken leg and arm and some cuts." Mr. Findeison patted his shoulder. "She's lucky it wasn't worse."

"Her face?" Seth couldn't stop thinking about all that red.

"The gash is this long," cried his mother. She held her shaking hands about four inches apart. "All the way across her forehead."

"It's stitched up," said Mr. Findeison. "She got smacked by a couple of tons of metal. Be glad she's alive."

"Did they tell you how it happened?" asked Seth.

"A car hit her. That's all I know," his father replied. "Captain Van Arkle's coming over to fill us in."

25

"I want to go to her," said Mrs. Findeison.

"They've got her doped up now, Fay. Let's wait until they take her to her room." Mr. Findeison turned to Seth. "How about getting your mother some coffee? There's a machine in the hall." He dug into his pocket for change.

His parents were gone when Seth returned to the waiting room. The receptionist directed him to the lounge at the end of the hall. The Findeisons sat at a formica coffee table across from Captain Van Arkle.

"She was crossing Main at Sixth Avenue about quarter to seven," Van Arkle was saying as Seth pulled up a chair.

"How could anyone do such a terrible thing?" Mrs. Findeison covered her face with her hands.

Van Arkle reached across the narrow table and touched her shoulder. "Would it be better if your husband and I talked alone?"

"No, please go on." She wiped her eyes. "This whole thing is so upsetting."

"I understand." The police chief took a small notebook from his pocket. "From what Hilary was able to tell us, she was about halfway across the intersection when the car hit her. Came out of nowhere, she says. She didn't see it coming, only remembers the sound of the muffler. The impact knocked her out, and she didn't regain consciousness until they got her to the hospital. We found the car against a telephone pole."

"You have the driver then?" Mr. Findeison asked.

"He was gone by the time the ambulance arrived,

26

but we picked him up at home. We knew the car."
Van Arkle took a sip of coffee from his Styrofoam
cup. "Frankly, we've had trouble with this guy before."

"You mean this isn't the first time?" Mr. Findeison
said.

"He never hurt anybody before. But the blood alcohol tests look decisive, and we're charging him with
D.W.I."

"What's that?" asked Seth.

"Driving while intoxicated," replied Van Arkle,
glancing at Seth for the first time. "Drunk driving."
He turned back to Seth's parents. "The new district
attorney is real tough on bodily injury cases. And we
got this guy solid. You might remember him," Van
Arkle said as he stood up. "He used to coach over at
the school. Max Hampton."

Seth caught his breath. His father looked at him.

Captain Van Arkle shook Mr. Findeison's hand.
"I'll keep in touch."

As soon as the policeman had left, Seth slumped
back in his chair. Why did it have to be Max? Max—
who'd let him join the Small Fry basketball team in
fourth grade, even though he was so much shorter
than everybody else. Max—who'd given him confidence that he could be a good player if he worked
hard and kept at it. Max—who'd taught him never to
give up until the last buzzer sounded. Why did Max
have to be the one who ran down his sister?

"How could it have been him?" murmured Seth.

"I know how you felt about him, son." His father

27

frowned. "But the truth is he's been a drunk for years, and now he's hurt someone."

"I'm going to the bathroom," Seth said.

"Are you feeling all right, dear?" his mother asked.

"Not really."

Seth skipped school the next day even though his mother encouraged him to go. She thought school would get his mind off the accident. Nothing could do that.

His parents were at the hospital all day Wednesday. Seth stayed home shooting baskets in the driveway until Mr. Gottshall got tired of the banging and asked him to stop. His father arrived home about 6:00. His mother decided to stay the night at the hospital because Hilary's leg was giving her a lot of pain.

When Seth came home after school Thursday, his parents were in the kitchen, huddled over the table. As soon as they saw him, they gathered up the papers strewn in front of them.

"What's all that stuff?" he asked.

"How was school?" Mr. Findeison said, stuffing his papers into a folder.

"Everybody wanted to know about the accident." Seth washed his hands in the sink. "Is everything all right? You guys look upset."

"I haven't slept for nearly three days," answered his mother, as she poured him a glass of milk. "You can't expect me to look my best."

"Hilary's much better today," said Mr. Findeison.

Seth gulped his milk. "Maybe I can go visit her now."

"We're going back tonight," he said. "You can come with us."

There was a knock at the front door. Mrs. Findeison jumped. "Who could that be?" she said.

"I'll go," said Seth, heading into the living room. When he opened the door, the last person he expected to see was Max Hampton.

The man stood on the porch, with his shoulders slumped and his hands stuck in his pants pockets. His forehead was bandaged. "Your parents home?" he asked. His voice was little more than a whisper.

Seth hesitated a moment, knowing Max was an unwelcome guest.

"I wanted them and you to know how sorry I am about your sister."

Mr. Findeison appeared in the doorway. "Hampton, you've done enough without bothering us at home."

"But it wasn't me that hit her," Max said, his voice louder now. "My car didn't hit her, I swear."

"Leave us alone!" Mr. Findeison slammed the door shut.

Seth backed away.

"He's gone," said his mother, as she peered out the window. "Why did he come here?"

"He wanted to say he was sorry," said Seth.

"If he's so sorry, why's he going to drag this through court for the next year? We didn't need more money problems," said Mr. Findeison.

"You said Max's insurance company would pay all the medical bills," said Seth.

"That was before he claimed it was another car

29

that hit her. The only problem is no one saw it but him, and *he* can't remember what it looked like." Mr. Findeison shook his head. "We won't see a dime until his trial's over."

"Don't get yourself worked up again, Roger," said Mrs. Findeison. "Captain Van Arkle said the case against Hampton is solid."

"And now the doctor's telling us that Hilary is going to need plastic surgery on her face," he continued.

"Seth," his mother said soothingly, "this isn't your problem. We'll work it out. Don't worry, okay?"

Don't worry, thought Seth. Fat chance.

He waited at Bryan's locker after his last period class the next day. He hadn't asked his friend for a favor in a long time, but he needed one now.

"How's Hilary?" Bryan said when he saw Seth. "Did she get my card?"

"Yeah, she showed it to me last night." He stepped aside so Bryan could open his locker. "You've got no class, man."

"I thought it was a great card. Come on, it made her laugh, didn't it?"

"Until she cried."

"So, is she better?" Bryan said, tugging his basketball out from the bottom of the locker.

"Her leg isn't hurting as much as the first couple days," Seth replied. "She has to stay in the hospital for a while, though. They've got her all rigged up. She looks like a grasshopper caught in a web."

"I'll tell her you said that." Bryan kicked his locker

30

door closed. "What lousy luck. Of all the streets in town, she has to be crossing that one exactly when Max the Lush comes barreling along."

"He says he didn't hit her."

Bryan snickered. "Oh right. That's why his car plowed into a pole two feet away from her."

"He tried to talk to my parents, but they slammed the door in his face," Seth said, as they elbowed their way through the crowd in the hall.

"I would've too," said Bryan. "He's got a lot of nerve."

Once they were outside on the front walk, Seth stopped. "Bry, I want to go see Max. I need to hear his side of the story. I owe it to him."

"Get serious." Bryan looked at him incredulously.

"I was hoping you'd come with me. It would make it easier for me if you would."

Bryan shook his head. "No way. I'm not getting mixed up in this."

"It'll only take a few minutes. You can spare a few minutes, can't you?" He rapped his knuckles on the ball under Bryan's arm.

"Do yourself a favor, buddy. Forget about Max. If he didn't do it, the police will clear him. If he did, he deserves what he gets." Bryan tossed him the ball. "You've got your own problems to worry about. Like making the team. It's got to be you and me that make that final cut, remember?"

"I thought I could count on you." Seth turned and walked toward the street, throwing the ball back over his shoulder. He didn't bother to check if Bryan caught it.

31

He should have seen it coming . . . should have realized everything between Bryan and him had changed. Making the team . . . that's what mattered to Bry and the others. Nothing could be allowed to interfere with that.

Seth knew the feeling. He had had it himself until the night his father came home with his last paycheck.

As Seth headed home, he wondered if he would have the nerve to visit Max, knowing he had to go without Bryan. Maybe it was crazy to want to talk to his old coach. After all, Hilary was lying in a hospital because of him. And the police said Max had been drunk. After smelling liquor on him when they met earlier in the week, Seth could believe it.

But what if Max's story was true, and he *hadn't* been the one who ran her down? What if he hit the telephone pole trying to avoid an accident that had happened before he came along?

Seth needed to know for sure. That was why he had to see Max, even if he had to go alone.

Chapter 4

After a weekend of listening to his parents and visiting relatives talk about "the drunk who tore up the face of our beautiful Hilary," Seth began to have second thoughts about seeing Max. If his family knew he was even considering going, they'd be furious—especially his father.

As he walked to school on Monday, Seth made up his mind to see what the police came up with before doing anything.

The weather was as gray as his mood. The leaves hung limply from the branches. The colors had changed overnight—not to bright reds and yellows, but to dull brown. A morning fog covered him with tiny droplets of cold moisture. He zipped his jacket and pulled up the hood.

It wasn't going to be a good day. He had first period P.E., and it was a sure bet that Coach would make them do laps around the soccer field through the tall, wet grass, and his shoes would get soaked. Then he had the usual Monday morning current events quiz in civics class. Unfortunately, the only current events he'd been aware of for the past week wouldn't be on it. Maybe, if he was lucky, he'd have time to cram for the math quiz he'd forgotten all about until breakfast that morning.

The last place Seth wanted to go after a day like that was Miss Nichol's house. She had called Sunday afternoon while he was at the hospital, asking if Seth could do some work for her. His mother said he would come the next day, even though she had no right to make plans for him. He let her know, too.

"But Miss Nichol is such a nice lady," his mother had said. "She asked about Hilary and offered to help if she could. What could I say?"

"That I would call her back," Seth replied, irritated.

"I suppose I could have. I just wasn't thinking. I've been preoccupied since the accident."

"I have a newspaper staff meeting after school."

"Can't you go to Miss Nichol's afterwards? We'll be late getting back from the hospital anyway."

"That's not the point, Mom." But he saw she was getting upset, so he let it drop.

By 3:30 the fog had lifted, and it was warm enough to shed his jacket. The day was no less dismal, however. The sky had turned the color of his once-white gym socks—the ones that got grayer every time they were washed.

Seth decided to walk by Sixth and Main on his way to Miss Nichol's, because he hadn't been there since the accident. He was surprised to see that, except for some faint skid marks and a scrape on the telephone pole, the corner looked as though nothing out of the ordinary had ever occurred there.

Not that he expected painted outlines of where Hilary had fallen or a dated commemorative plaque describing the event. But it didn't seem right that someone could be mangled there, and you couldn't even tell.

He jogged the two blocks to Miss Nichol's house, which sat on a knoll above the sidewalk near the Main Street traffic light. It was one of the oldest houses in town—at least that's what Phoebe claimed.

As soon as his foot touched Miss Nichol's porch, he heard yaps and scratching on the door. When the door opened, Babette charged, nipping at his ankles.

"Naughty girl. Seth is a friend," scolded Miss Nichol, tapping the poodle's snout. "So good to see you. We've been waiting." She picked up Babette and gestured for him to enter.

Inside it was dark and too warm. The windows in the living room to his right were covered with heavy drapes. He could barely see past the shadows into the small room on his left. The only light filtered down the hallway from the rear of the house.

"Place your things there," said Miss Nichol, pointing to the small table beside the door. "My blood isn't ready for this cold yet. I turned on the furnace today and got out Babette's winter sweater." She smoothed a wrinkle in the pink knitted band on the dog's back.

As Seth put his books down, he saw Phoebe's French horn case standing on the floor next to the ceramic umbrella stand. Maybe the day wouldn't be a total waste after all.

At that moment, Phoebe appeared in the hallway,

her hands and apron covered with flour. "Hi, Seth. I've been helping Auntie bake."

"She insisted on volunteering today for some reason." Miss Nichol winked at him.

"I'd better check the bread," Phoebe said, hurrying back to the kitchen. Babette jumped from Miss Nichol's arms and followed, her claws making click-click sounds on the wood floor.

"Oh my, I've embarrassed her," sighed Miss Nichol. "It's been so long since I . . ." She waved her long delicate fingers in the air as if she were chasing away an annoying fly. "Well, I should know better, that's all. Let's get to work, shall we?"

Before Seth could reply, she took his arm and escorted him up the carpeted staircase. Upstairs, the hall floor was covered by a narrow pink carpet. For its entire length, the middle of the rose pattern was worn to a grayish white. Although most of the rooms were hidden behind closed doors, two, a bedroom and a bathroom with pink seahorse wallpaper, were open. Sunshine streamed through their windows into the hallway, making it brighter than downstairs.

Seth followed Miss Nichol to the last room on the left. As she pushed open the door, cool air rushed toward them. Its smell made him remember the story hours he and Hilary used to attend at the public library when they were little. A massive desk sat under the window. The other three walls were covered with rows of books from ceiling to floor.

"My father, Phoebe's great-grandfather, was an attorney. Most of these were his books." She ran a finger over the spines. "My goodness! I must dust these off."

She crossed the room to a ladder-back chair in the corner. "My father used this at his desk, but lately I've come to prefer my cushioned chair. I want his stored in the attic."

Seth lifted the wooden chair. "How do I get up there?"

"No, no. First the rungs need regluing."

"I thought you didn't want to use it anymore," said Seth.

"Now tell me, young man, what would be the sense of storing a broken chair?"

Seth shrugged uncertainly.

She handed him the glue. "I'll leave the door open so you get some heat. The radiator's turned off in here."

It didn't take Seth long to finish the job. Just as he wiped off the last of the excess glue, Miss Nichol reappeared. "Good. You've finished. Next I need the coleus plants brought in from the back porch. With this weather, we're due for a frost, and I'll lose every one."

She led him down the back staircase, descending briskly, despite her age. The passage was narrow and unlighted, and there was no railing to hold. The warm smell of fresh bread filled the staircase and made his stomach growl.

They emerged in the kitchen. Babette raced into Miss Nichol's arms, then barked angrily when she spied Seth. Phoebe stood by the sink, drying baking pans.

Walking past the counter covered with golden brown bread and several varieties of cookies, Seth's stomach growled again, this time more loudly.

"You'll get some when the work is complete," said Miss Nichol, smiling.

Nearly forty-five minutes passed before he returned to the kitchen. There had been a dozen coleus and geranium pots to move, as well as four hanging spider plants. Then Miss Nichol directed him to get out a ladder and hang her bird feeder on a limb of the spruce tree. Finally, he had to pull the dried-up bean and tomato plants from the vegetable garden and cart them to a compost pile behind the shed.

"Chocolate chip, molasses, or macaroons?" asked Phoebe, when Seth came back inside.

"Macaroons." He sat down at the table under the window. A vase of peach-colored gladioli sat on the windowsill next to him. He knew what they were because his father had planted them one summer. "That's my favorite flower," he said to Miss Nichol. "Maybe because they grow tall."

"Like you," Phoebe added, finishing his thought. They both chuckled.

"That's the last of the season. I miss the flowers when they're over," said Miss Nichol, handing him a glass of milk. "Do your parents still have that lovely garden out front?"

"Not this year."

"Those marigolds your father planted along the sidewalk were always so attractive," she continued.

"I liked them, too." Suddenly, he felt very sad.

Phoebe sat down across from him and passed the

38

plate of cookies. Aware that she was watching, he took a bite of a macaroon. Not up to his mother's standards, but not bad.

"Good," he mumbled as he chewed.

"My Phoebe is a girl of many talents," said Miss Nichol.

"Oh, Auntie," moaned Phoebe, blushing.

Seth couldn't believe it. This was the girl who hadn't flinched when he told her the dirtiest locker room joke he'd ever heard. The girl who hadn't batted an eye the summer when she dove in McNeal's pond with ten kids watching and her bathing suit came off. The girl who, in all the years he'd known her, never, ever had the pink of embarrassment creep into her cheeks. Now she was turning scarlet because of a little compliment about her cooking.

"I can't tell you how I appreciate your help, Seth," said Miss Nichol, holding a doggie treat between her fingers. With head tilted back, Babette hopped on her hind legs under the woman's hand.

"More?" Phoebe pushed the plate of cookies across the table. Seth took two.

"I hate to bother Phoebe's dad with the small tasks. He does so much for me already. I probably make things more difficult for myself—not to mention my family—by refusing to drive."

"You don't drive?" Seth asked.

"I lived in Boston for forty years and never had a car. Never needed one. And I'm too old to learn to drive now." The white-haired woman patted Babette's head. "In my opinion, the trouble an automobile causes far outweighs its usefulness."

"My sister would agree with you," said Seth glumly.

"Yes, my point exactly." Miss Nichol wiped her hands on her apron. "Your sister—is she better?"

"She's coming home at the end of the week." He didn't think he should mention her face.

"Good, good," Miss Nichol murmured.

"Imagine it being Max Hampton, of all people," said Phoebe.

"Oh, did you know him, dear?" asked Miss Nichol.

"Sure. He used to be the gym teacher in elementary school."

Miss Nichol glanced at Seth. "Then Mr. Hampton must have been your teacher, too."

He nodded. "And my coach."

"I didn't realize. What an unfortunate coincidence."

"What's going to happen to him?" asked Phoebe.

"The police told my parents he might go to jail since it was the third time he got caught drunk driving," replied Seth. Thinking about Max took his hunger away. He put down his cookie.

"Don't worry," said Miss Nichol, placing her hand on his shoulder. "I have faith in the fairness of the legal system." She clapped her hands and Babette ran to her. "Now if you'll excuse me, I have some correspondence to complete. Seth, I'll see you in a couple days after the glue on the chair dries. There are a few other items you can take to the attic then."

"Okay, Miss Nichol." He stood up.

"Your money for today is on the counter."

"Thanks," Seth called as she left the kitchen. He turned to Phoebe. "I wish I could take her advice."

"About what?" asked Phoebe.

"Not worrying." He sighed. "It's such a mess—Hilary, Max, my dad. Everything. If only . . ."

"If only what?"

"Never mind." He shrugged as he took the money from the counter and stuffed it into his pocket. "Guess I'll see you later."

"There's one more macaroon . . . if you want it, that is." She held out the plate.

"They were great. Really." Then, biting the cookie so she'd know he hadn't taken it just to be polite, Seth hurried out the back door.

Chapter 5

"Seth, are you home?"

Swearing under his breath, he opened his bedroom door. "Up here, Mom," he called down. Her note said they would be gone until 6:00, and it was only 4:00. He was annoyed at being disturbed when he was enjoying the quiet of an empty house.

"Come down here, so I don't have to shout."

Seth flipped his pencil onto his new desk. He had just started the cartoon about the new cheerleader uniforms that Jeff Baker, the layout editor, asked him to finish by Wednesday. He didn't welcome the interruption. "What?" he said, as he descended the steps.

"Don't use that tone of voice with me," Mrs. Findeison said. "We've driven to every hospital supply place within thirty miles looking for a wheelchair for Hilary, and I'm not in the mood." She pulled an envelope from her purse. "You'd think we could find a common thing like that anywhere, but you'd be wrong." She handed Seth the envelope.

"What's this for?"

"My babysitting money from last week. I didn't get

43

it to the bank yesterday, and we need the deposit to cover the check I just wrote.''

"So, what am I supposed to do with it?''

"You'll have to take this up to the bank before it closes.'' She snapped her purse closed. "Your father's waiting for me in the car. We have to be at the hospital by 4:30 to talk to the doctor. We'll be late as it is.''

"Mom, I have a deadline tomorrow. I was in the middle of—''

"It won't take you more than twenty minutes.'' She flew out the door before he could argue. "And put the chicken in the oven at 5:30,'' she called from the sidewalk.

The bank was jammed, of course. A twenty-minute errand, she said. More like two hours by the looks of it. Counting bodies and sizing up the customers, Seth chose what he thought would be the fastest of the four lines. Several minutes later—after the lines on either side had advanced and his hadn't—he realized his guess had been wrong. He glanced at the clock on the wall behind the counter and silently cursed his mother for not doing this herself.

The mention of a familiar name caught his attention. Turning, he saw the teller at the next window greeting a woman in a wheelchair.

"How are you this afternoon, Mrs. Prescott?'' the teller said cheerfully.

Without replying, the woman laid a piece of paper on the counter. Her gray hair was perfectly arranged, and she wore a tailored navy blue suit. From her ap-

44

pearance and the teller's behavior, Seth knew it was the same Mrs. Prescott who lived in the big Victorian house . . . whose desk now sat in his room . . . who had the Neanderthal for a nephew.

He had never seen her before—only heard rumors about her money and influence around town. He was surprised by the wheelchair.

"Beautiful day, isn't it?" said the middle-aged teller, as he typed on his computer terminal. "Account number, please."

"It's on the slip," she replied.

"That was quite a bit of excitement over on your side of town last Tuesday morning," continued the teller, seeming not to notice the impatience in her voice.

"Excitement?" asked Mrs. Prescott.

"I was referring to that accident where the young woman was struck by a car."

"Why no, I didn't know about it," said Mrs. Prescott. "I've been away since Labor Day. I only returned this morning and haven't read the papers yet."

"You had a pleasant trip, I hope." He pulled a handful of cash from his drawer.

"Yes, it was an enjoyable stay. I flew to New York to visit some friends."

Leaning across the counter, the teller reached down and placed the money, bill by bill, into her outstretched hand. "Twenty, forty, sixty, eighty . . ."

"Next," said the teller for Seth's line.

The person behind him nudged Seth's back. Embarrassed, he quickly stepped forward.

45

By the time Seth deposited his mother's money, Mrs. Prescott had left the bank. When he went outside, he spotted her wheeling herself down the sidewalk toward the post office next door.

Seth headed the other way.

He was almost past the silver Mercedes before he noticed it, parked two cars from the corner. For a moment he froze, staring at the car. His first thought was to run—like a cheetah. But he couldn't resist looking at the damage his desk had made.

Not seeing Weber anywhere, Seth circled around the front of the Mercedes to the driver's side. Strange. He couldn't find the scratch. Thinking the sun's glare had camouflaged the mark, he bent down to examine it more carefully.

He couldn't believe it. The shiny finish was unmarred. The scratch was gone!

Bewildered, Seth peered in the windows at the interior. He wondered if it was a different silver Mercedes, although he knew that was unlikely since he had just seen Mrs. Prescott. A map lay across the passenger seat. As he craned his neck to see more, he felt a tight grip on his shoulder.

"What do you think you're doing?"

Seth swung around and looked up into Weber's glaring black eyes.

"Hey, you're the kid that took the desk, aren't you?" he said gruffly, stuffing a fresh pack of cigarettes into his shirt pocket.

"Yes," Seth replied uncomfortably. It was a public place. The guy wouldn't dare pull anything. Just the same, Seth stepped away from the car and out of Weber's reach. "I was admiring your car. Uh, what wax do you use? It looks real nice."

"Get out of my way." Weber jerked open the car door. "I warned you once to keep away from my car. There better not be a next time."

Sputtering loudly, the engine turned over, and the Mercedes pulled out of the parking space. The diesel engine's exhaust fumes made Seth cough. He watched as Weber swung in front of the post office to pick up Mrs. Prescott.

He didn't know whether to be relieved or worried. Weber had fixed the scratch, yet he didn't act as if he suspected Seth of putting it there. How long would it take him to figure it out? Seeing Seth around the car again was sure to help Weber make the connection, no matter how dumb he was.

It wouldn't be bad if all he had to do was pay a few bucks for touch-up paint. But Seth had a feeling that Owen Weber wasn't the type to settle things that way.

He didn't want to think about it.

When he arrived home, Seth could no longer concentrate on the newspaper cartoon. His mind was on other subjects—Weber, the missing scratch, Hilary's accident, and especially Max.

After fifteen minutes of doodling, Seth gave up on the new cheerleader outfits. In spite of his earlier decision to put off his visit to his former coach, he realized he couldn't wait any longer.

After looking up Max's address in the phone book, Seth grabbed his jacket and started out the front door.

Then, remembering his mother's instructions, he jogged back to the kitchen, switched on the oven, and slid in the roasting chicken. His parents wouldn't be home for an hour. They'd never know he'd gone out or where he'd been.

Max's apartment house was on Second Avenue near the railroad station and most of the town's bars. Not the best of neighborhoods, as his mother would say. It was a three-story, wood-frame building that looked as if it hadn't been painted since World War II.

After chaining his bike to the trash dumpster in the side yard, the most secure structure he could find, Seth climbed the crumbling concrete steps and entered the building.

A single light bulb at the end of a cord dangled from the entryway ceiling like a pendulum. When he pushed the front door closed, the light began to swing, casting eerie, vibrating shadows on the peeling walls.

Twelve black metal mailboxes lined the wall above the radiator. Seth could barely read the smudged, handprinted names and apartment numbers in the dim light. At last he deciphered Max's.

It was on the second floor at the back of the building. Seth had to maneuver around cardboard boxes and plastic trash bags piled outside the apartment doors. The sour smell of garbage mingled with the odors of cooking and cigar smoke that drifted into the hall.

Max opened his door after the third knock. "What

48

are you doing here?'' he said, as he tucked his undershirt into his pants.

"I'm sorry about the way my father treated you at the house.''

"Well, I'll be . . .'' Max shook his head. Then, grinning, he opened the door all the way. "Want to come in?''

"I don't want to interrupt anything,'' Seth said, stepping inside.

"Interrupt? That's a laugh.'' Max shut the door. "I was just throwing together some dinner. Can I get you anything?''

"No. I'll be eating soon.'' Seth was relieved not to smell alcohol on Max the way he had in front of Genuardi's store the time they spoke.

He looked around the apartment. It was a single room with a stove, refrigerator, and table in one corner and an unmade bed in the other. A tan sofa and television sat near the middle, centered on an oval rug. Several cans and dirty pots were piled in the sink.

"I probably shouldn't have come by,'' Max said. "Can't blame them for not wanting to talk to me.''

"They're just upset. They've been having a bad time for a while. This accident set them off.''

Max nodded. "I understand.'' He gestured for Seth to sit down.

"I can't stay long.'' Seth stepped onto the oval rug, but remained standing. "What *really* happened, Max? I need to hear it from you.''

"It wasn't me that hit your sister, Seth.'' Max lowered himself onto the sofa. "There was another car. I told the police about it, but they think I was seeing

49

pink elephants. Nobody believes a drunk, you know.''

Seth shifted his weight and stared at his feet. He couldn't look at Max while he asked his next question. ''Why'd you run away then, if you weren't the one?''

''I don't know how I ended up back here. Can't remember any of it. I was dazed, maybe because of my head.'' He touched the small bandage on his forehead.

''I'm telling you, though, Hilary was already down on the ground when I saw her,'' Max continued. ''I had to swerve to keep from running over her. That's when I hit the pole. There was another car driving away. I didn't see it—at least I don't remember if I did—since I had my eyes on her lying in the street. But I heard it. That's the truth.''

''Didn't the police try to find the other car?'' asked Seth.

''Oh, they checked all the houses around for witnesses. But it was early in the morning and nobody saw the accident. And they couldn't find that woman.''

''What woman?''

''The one who called the ambulance, then hung up without giving her name. She probably didn't see it happen anyway.''

''But you were drunk, Max. The police said you were when they found you.''

The man shook his head. ''Not when I was driving. I was sober then. I'd been trying to get off the bottle, really I had. So hard. But I just wasn't thinking right that morning.

"When I got back here after hitting that pole, I knew it looked bad for me and nobody was going to believe me. And I said to myself, 'Just one drink to calm my nerves. That's all.' But then I had another. I don't know how many. And next thing I know, there's the police at the door." He stared at Seth. "Nothing I can do about the police now. I told them what happened and that's that. But I don't want *you* to think I hurt your sister. You believe me, don't you?"

Seth hesitated, not sure how to answer—hesitated too long.

Max's shoulders slumped forward.

Maybe the story was farfetched, thought Seth. Coming from anyone else, he'd dismiss it just as the police had. But not from Max. Max had always been honest with his players. Even that time when his wife was so sick and he forgot to show up for a game and they had to forfeit. Max never made excuses, never tried to wiggle out of it. He stood in front of the team the next day and said he'd screwed up and was sorry and it would never happen again. It hadn't.

If Max claimed there was another car, it was because he truly believed there was.

Seth sat down next to him. "Don't you have a lawyer?"

"Some young public defender fresh out of law school. The court assigned him to me because I couldn't afford my own."

"Isn't he supposed to help you?"

"He's got ninety-nine other cases. I don't matter to him." Max shrugged. "He wants me to plead guilty and get the whole thing over with."

"But you said you were innocent," said Seth.

"He claims no jury will believe that. He figures if I plead and agree to go into alcohol counseling, the judge might go easier on me. A fine, probation, and suspended license. I don't feel much like driving again anyway."

There was a darkness in Max's face. Seth had seen it before. On the faces of basketball players when they were twenty points down with only two minutes left in the game. On kids' faces when they opened their last report card of the year to bad news. On his father's face ever since he lost his job. It was the look people got when they thought it was all over, when they decided to give up. Defeat.

"But if there was another car, then someone out there hit my sister and let you take the blame." Seth rubbed his palms over the knees of his jeans.

The man stood up. "Look, I'll be fine. You just take care of your sister."

"I wish it hadn't been you," said Seth, as they walked toward the door.

"Thanks, son." Max reached out to shake his hand, holding on as though he were afraid Seth would slip away forever when he released his grip.

Chapter 6

Seth got home just in time to witness his parents fighting about the Five Little Monsters—his father saying he hated having them around, his mother insisting they needed them to pay the bills.

He burrowed under his covers that night knowing there could have been money, and his father could have been working at the mill instead of watching cartoons, and his mother could have been cooking her sponge cake surprise instead of diapering five smelly brats. Everything could have been fine if he hadn't lied about the phone call.

By the next afternoon, the only thing that Seth had found to get his mind off all of it was doing math homework. It was like pinching his thigh when the dentist worked on his teeth. The pain in his leg made him forget the one in his mouth.

He was halfway through the math assignment when he heard a knock on the back door. He raised the window and peered down.

"I've got a pan of lasagna from my mother," Phoebe said, looking up at him. "It's frozen, so your mom can use it any time."

"They're at the hospital now, but the door's

open." He shut the window, then hurriedly stashed the dirty underwear and socks on the floor into a drawer. As he plopped down on his bed again, he heard her coming up, two steps at a time. "Don't you ever walk?" he said, as Phoebe entered his room.

"Sometimes." She pulled out his desk chair and sat down. "I put the lasagna in the freezer. What are you doing?"

"Algebra. I flunked the first two quizzes. I have to ace tomorrow's or my guidance counselor will call my parents. They don't need that now."

"Maybe I'd better leave so you can study."

He tossed the book aside. "You don't have to. I need a break."

Phoebe smiled, then turned toward the wall where he had hung his favorite drawings. "These are wonderful, especially the one of the Sachem Creek Covered Bridge."

"Thanks."

"Remember the unicorn with butterflies flitting around it?" she said. "You drew it for me after that dog killed my rabbit."

He nodded. It was the first drawing he ever gave away. He'd been ten.

"I have it on my bulletin board. It cheers me up."

"You kept it all this time?"

"Sure. It meant a lot to me." She paused. "Still does."

"Yeah?" Seth liked the thought of her looking at it every day. "I haven't done any drawings like that for a while."

"I thought you were doing cartoons for the school paper," she said.

"I didn't mean cartoons. For those, someone tells me what to draw, and I do it." He glanced at the flowing willow tree sketch on the wall. "But when an idea comes to me, and I turn it into a picture, it's . . . well, that's when it's the best. I feel great when I finish." Lowering his eyes, he picked at a loose thread on his bedspread. "I haven't felt that way lately."

Seth knew she was watching him, but he couldn't look up. He was afraid she'd question him until he told her why nothing was the same since his dad stopped working. And why he couldn't concentrate on basketball the way he used to. And why even drawing, which had always been his refuge from problems, couldn't raise his spirits. Yet a part of him wanted to tell her everything.

The room was silent except for the hum of his clock.

"Don't worry," Phoebe said brightly. "I know you'll draw that way again soon. Maybe when basketball season starts. You always do so well. And Hilary will be all right by then. You're bound to feel better about everything."

"I'm not so sure," he said.

"Are you worried about tryouts? Because you shouldn't be. You're better than Lee or Bryan or any of them. You'll make varsity, I know it."

But at that moment, for the first time, Seth realized that he wasn't sure he *wanted* to make varsity, or even junior varsity. In fact, he wasn't sure he ever wanted to play the game again. Basketball was the reason that he made his father lose his job.

Even if the thought of playing didn't knot his stomach, and even if he could concentrate on his game long enough to make the cut, maybe he didn't deserve to be on the team and hear crowds cheer when he made a basket. Maybe he ought to quit right then and there.

"Can I help?" Phoebe said, dragging him out of his thoughts.

"Help with what? My algebra? I doubt you could make much sense of this stuff either."

"I wasn't thinking of your homework, Seth." She stepped over to the bed. "Have you heard this one?" she said, grinning. "Knock, knock."

Seth groaned. "Those are so dumb."

"Come on. Play along."

"Okay," he said. "Who's there?"

"Apple."

"Phoebe, I know that one."

"How about this? Knock, knock."

"Who's there?"

"Boo."

"Boo who?" He rolled his eyes. "Very bad."

"All right, all right. You're a tough case." She pushed up the sleeves of her sweater. "I know how to deal with you, Seth Findeison."

And she was on him, tickling his waist, under his arms, his neck. He fell back on his bed, laughing uncontrollably. She laughed, too, and tears ran down her cheeks.

At last she stopped. "Why did you do that?" he asked.

"I wanted you to laugh. I thought it would make you feel better."

"It worked."

"I almost forgot what I wanted to tell you," she said, jumping off the bed. "Auntie says the glue's dry on the chair, and she's ready for you to come back."

"I meant to go yesterday, but my mother had me running all over." Seth ran his fingers through his mussed blond hair.

"I have a message for Hilary from the twins, too. They say 'get well soon,' " she said, as she examined his drawings again. "They called from college last night. We told them Hilary was doing fine."

"Well, not quite." He pulled the algebra book from under his back and took it to the desk.

Phoebe looked over at him. "You said on Monday that she was coming home this week."

"I didn't want to mention the rest in front of your aunt," said Seth. "She's going to need plastic surgery. My parents are in a real snit over paying for it, too. They're afraid Max's trial will tie up the insurance money." He turned his back to her and rolled down the desk top. "But I don't think they have to worry about that happening."

"You went to see Max Hampton, didn't you?" Phoebe said. "I knew you would."

Phoebe seemed to understand things about him that no one else did. He never needed to explain to her why he hated swimming near the Black Rock Dam or why he walked home the long way some days.

Phoebe figured it out, the same way she knew he had to talk to Max about the accident.

Sighing, he leaned against the closed desk. "Max says somebody else hit Hilary before he came along."

"You're kidding."

"When I first heard it, I didn't know whether to believe him or not. I thought he was imagining it. Or maybe he was so upset that he started to believe he hadn't hit her."

"Or maybe he made it all up so the police would let him go," added Phoebe.

"Not Max," said Seth. "He always told us to stand up and take what we deserved. He wouldn't lie to save his skin." He paused a moment, mulling over the conversation he'd had with his former coach. "Talking to him made me think there *was* a second car."

Phoebe crossed the room to his side. "So, what happened to it?"

"That's the problem. Max says it drove off before the ambulance arrived. The police are sure Max was the one who hit Hilary."

"Then what did you mean about your parents not needing to worry about a trial?" asked Phoebe.

"Max's lawyer wants him to plead guilty. I think he will, too. He doesn't think anyone will ever believe him." Seth dug his hands into his pockets. "He shouldn't be convicted of something he didn't do. I wish I could help him."

"I don't see what *you* could do."

But Seth barely heard her. Max had mentioned something the day before, and it gave him an idea.

"I don't know anybody who didn't like Max, except some of those prissies who hated sweating," said Phoebe. "Everybody pitched in for flowers when his wife died. My father thinks the school board was unfair, kicking him out like that. I mean, I never saw him drinking at school, did you? Seth, are you listening?"

"Maybe I *can* do something to help."

"Like what?"

"There was a woman who might have seen the accident," he said. "She called the ambulance, but the police don't know who she was. If I can find her, maybe she can support Max's story."

"How are you going to do that if the police couldn't?"

Seth reached under the bed for his shoes. "Maybe they didn't look very hard because they didn't believe Max in the first place. And maybe they didn't ask the right people," he said, tying his laces. "Come on, we're going to visit your aunt."

"I don't see what good talking to Auntie will do," said Phoebe on the way to Miss Nichol's house.

"She might have seen someone that morning," said Seth. "In fact, she might have been the mystery caller herself."

"Auntie wouldn't let an innocent man be accused. She would have told the police if she'd seen anything."

"It's worth a try," Seth replied, as they crossed Main Street.

59

They found Miss Nichol at her kitchen table repotting coleus plants. "You're back," she said.

"Seth came to move the chair," said Phoebe. "And Mom asked me to pick up that knitting magazine."

"I see." Miss Nichol smiled, wiping her hands on a towel. "Let me show Seth the way. I'll be right down, dear."

He followed her up the narrow back stairs to the second floor. "Watch that you don't hit the woodwork," Miss Nichol directed, as he lifted the chair. She stood at the bottom of the attic stairs watching him carry it up. "Gently now," she called. "Use that sheet in the corner. Be sure to cover the chair completely."

"It's just how you want it," he said, when he came back down.

"Fine. Now I have one more thing I'd like you to do on Saturday," she said, stepping into the study.

"Saturday?" Seth asked.

"Is Saturday inconvenient?"

"No, Saturday's all right," he replied, glad for the chance to earn extra money.

"Good." She pointed to several cartons piled on the floor next to the radiator. "I'm sorting through my books. I'll have you take them to the attic, too."

She closed the study door, and they headed down the hall.

"I was wondering, Miss Nichol," began Seth, when they reached the back staircase. "Maybe you could help me . . . actually, help a friend of mine. It's about my sister's accident."

"Of course, any way I can. What is it?"

"You probably read in the newspaper about the woman who called the ambulance. The police think she might have seen the accident. But she—"

"And you think I was that woman."

"Well, I thought maybe since you take morning walks . . ."

"A logical conclusion. But not an accurate one," said Miss Nichol. "Babette and I saw the ambulance and all the activity on Main Street when we took our daily constitutional that morning. The sirens upset Babette terribly. But unfortunately that isn't what you mean, is it?"

"No. I was hoping you had seen the accident happen."

"I'm afraid not, Seth. If I had, I certainly would have told the police."

"That's what Phoebe said," he said.

Miss Nichol smiled.

"It might help Max—Max Hampton—if we could find that woman," said Seth.

"Yes, I heard some talk about your Mr. Hampton claiming his wasn't the car that struck her." She started down the staircase. "I'm sorry, Seth. I do wish I could help."

Phoebe was waiting in the kitchen. She didn't mention the accident until after Miss Nichol had given her the knitting magazine and she and Seth were outside on the sidewalk. "What did she say?"

"Looks like your aunt can't help find the witness," said Seth, kicking a stone.

"I told you as much. You wouldn't believe me."

"I kept hoping she had seen the accident and could support Max's story," he said, clenching his fist.

Phoebe patted his shoulder. "I know you're disappointed. Me, too. But we'll find a way to help Max."

"*We?*" He stopped walking.

"Unless you don't want my help." Phoebe raised her eyebrows.

"Do I have any choice?"

"Of course not." She laughed. "I have an idea. The morning newspaper carriers deliver about the time the accident happened."

"I didn't think of that."

"John Martin does the part of town where Hilary was hit. Maybe he saw the woman. I'll ask him tomorrow morning when we pick up the papers."

"You don't have to do this, Phoebe."

"I want to." She smiled at him, then stuck the knitting magazine in her backpack. "I'd better get home."

"Hey, wait," Seth called, after she had walked a few yards. He ran to catch up. "Want to go to The Spot for a Whiz Bang, like we used to?"

"You still drink that fizzy stuff?"

"Sure. Well?"

She stared at him for a long minute. "It's getting close to dinner. I really have to go."

It was no big deal. So why did he feel disappointed?

"How about after school tomorrow?" she added.

"Then I can tell you what John said about the accident."

"Good. I'll see you then." He waved as she walked away. He couldn't help grinning.

Chapter 7

When he saw the group coming across the soccer field, Seth regretted telling Phoebe to meet him on the bleachers. The dismissal bell in the junior high building had just rung. She would be there any minute.

"Why are you hanging around here?" asked Bryan, approaching the bleachers.

"Yeah, Findeison, who are you waiting for?" Lee taunted.

"Nobody. Is there a law against sitting here?" He wished the guys would take off.

"Nobody, eh?" said Jon. "Word has it our boy's been holding out on us. I hear he found himself a girlfriend."

"You heard wrong," said Seth.

"Phoebe Nichol, *I* heard." Lee jabbed Seth's side with his elbow. "Isn't that right, buddy?"

"I'm not waiting for anybody, *buddy*." Seth said, climbing off the bleachers. As he strode across the field, away from the junior high building, he heard them snickering. He hoped Phoebe hadn't seen him.

He started to walk home. But a thought, which had

65

been nagging at him since the day before, made him change his plans. Instead, he headed across town.

He couldn't get the silver Mercedes out of his mind. It wasn't only nervousness about the scratch. There was something else—he couldn't quite put his finger on what—that made him want to take another look at the car.

As he crept into the bushes behind the Prescott barn, he realized that what he was doing was risky, illegal, and probably not too smart. But if he hurried, he figured he could get in and out of the barn with no problem. The window next to him was hidden from view by brush and evergreens, so no one in the house could see him. He had scouted the yard, and it was deserted.

Taking a deep breath, Seth pushed up the window. The bushes behind him rustled. Startled, he nearly put his hand through the glass. He spun around and bumped headlong into Phoebe.

"Are you crazy, sneaking around this place?" she said.

"Not so loud." He clamped his hand over her mouth. "What are you doing here?"

"Following you." Her eyes narrowed. "Why didn't you wait for me?"

Good question.

Because some guys teased me, and I didn't want them to see you with me, he thought.

Bad answer.

Being with Phoebe felt better than sinking a half-court shot in the final seconds of a tie game. He wasn't sure why he tried to hide that from the guys.

66

And he didn't know how to explain his actions to her.

She waited for his reply, her eyes searching his face. "I'm going," she said finally.

Maybe she found her answer, or maybe she gave up. Seth couldn't tell.

"In case you're interested," she added, "John Martin was no help. By the time he came along on his paper route, the police and ambulance were already there."

Seth grabbed her arm and pulled her back. "Don't go off mad."

"I'm not mad. But I *am* going. Owen Weber gives me the creeps. I don't ever want to see him, his car, or that scratch again."

"The scratch is gone," said Seth.

"Good," said Phoebe. "Let's get out of here before he catches us and makes us pay for fixing it."

"That's just the point," he whispered, leaning close to her. "I saw him a couple days ago near the bank. He recognized me. He *had* to know the desk scratched his car that morning, but he never said a word. It doesn't make sense."

"So what? The guy is strange. We already knew that." She started into the bushes. "We're off the hook. Let's not push our luck."

"Wait. Do me a favor?" He pointed to the corner of the barn facing the house. "Stand over there out of sight and watch for Weber. Tap on the window if he comes toward the barn."

Phoebe scrunched up her nose. "You'll owe me for this one."

He grinned. "How about another Whiz Bang? And this time I'll wait for you."

She hesitated a moment. "Okay, but make it snappy."

Seth climbed through the open window onto the top of a workbench inside the barn. In the dim light, he saw the silver Mercedes sitting in the middle of the floor, its headlights facing the street. Hopping off the bench, he circled the car to the front right fender. As he knelt down and ran his fingers over the area where the deep scratch had been, his heart skipped a beat. The paint was as smooth as glass.

Remembering the map he'd seen two days before, he opened the driver's door. The map still lay on the passenger seat. As Seth reached for it, he flinched. "Ouch!"

"What happened?"

The voice made Seth jump. "Stop sneaking up on me," he said, as Phoebe hopped off the workbench.

"Are you all right?" she asked.

"A lever by the steering wheel poked me." He rubbed his shoulder. "You were supposed to keep watch."

"I wanted to see. I'm as much to blame for that scratch as you are." She stuck her head inside the car. "What's that?"

Seth held it under the car's interior light. "A map of Delaware." He reached across the seat and opened the glove compartment.

"Don't do that," Phoebe whispered.

"I'll put everything back," he replied, pulling out

68

some other maps and papers. He held them under the light. "Take a look at this. It's a receipt from a body shop and it's dated last week."

Phoebe gasped as she read it. "It cost that much? Are we ever in trouble if he decides to come after us! I didn't think the desk did that much damage."

"It didn't. Look at this." He handed the slip to Phoebe. "'Replace headlight and fender, pound out dent, paint.'"

"Weber went all the way to Wilmington to have it done." She glanced at Seth. "Why would he bother going so far just for—?"

A clanging sound outside interrupted her.

"Hide behind the car," whispered Seth, gently pushing the car door closed.

Moments later, the side door of the barn opened. A shaft of sunlight cut across the floor toward them. They crouched lower. Peering underneath the car, Seth watched a pair of large brown boots entering the building. He held his breath, afraid to make the slightest sound. He prayed the man wouldn't come closer to their hiding place.

A fluorescent light over the workbench flickered on. Weber dropped a metal object onto the bench and began striking it with a hammer. Seth's knees ached from the awkward position, but he didn't dare move. Phoebe squeezed his hand.

After several long minutes, the light flicked off and Weber left the barn, leaving the door open.

Seth signaled toward the window. "Hurry, before he comes back."

Staying low behind the car, the two friends crept to the rear of the barn. They were almost to the workbench, when Phoebe's arm brushed against some tools hanging on the wall. Before she could catch it, a rake fell to the floor with a clatter.

Seconds later, Owen Weber's huge bulk filled the entrance. "Hey!" he shouted, as he switched on the overhead light.

Seth and Phoebe ran for the window.

"What have you got there? Give me that, girl!"

"Hand me the receipt, Phoebe," yelled Seth, as Weber rushed toward them. "That's what he's after!"

But before Phoebe could react, Weber seized her around the waist, dragging her off the workbench. She kicked and twisted, but his grip was strong.

While Weber struggled to get the paper from her hand, Seth circled behind him and rammed his fist into the man's lower back. Caught off-guard, Weber loosened his hold on Phoebe. She wriggled out of his arms and ran for the side door.

As she escaped his grasp, Weber swung his powerful arm, knocking Seth to the floor. Then he went after Phoebe again.

At the moment Weber ran past him, Seth stuck out his leg. The man tripped and fell to his knees. Seth jumped up and raced to the open door where Phoebe waited. Grabbing her hand, he yanked her out of the barn. "This way. Over the fence," he shouted.

Looking over her shoulder, Phoebe screamed, "Seth, he has a pitchfork!"

They dashed across the lawn, cutting through a flower bed. Weber's feet pounded close behind.

When they reached the wooden rail fence, Seth scrambled over. He had run several feet into the neighbor's yard when he realized that Phoebe wasn't beside him. He turned around and saw her teetering on the top of the fence.

"Run!" he called to her. "Weber's right behind you."

"I can't!" she cried, as she climbed back down the fence into the Prescott yard. "I dropped the receipt."

Then, as Seth watched in horror, Weber ran toward her with his pitchfork raised high.

Chapter 8

With a quick thrust of his pitchfork, Weber stabbed the receipt which lay on the ground a few feet from Phoebe. She stopped in her tracks, then turned and raced to the fence.

"You kids will be sorry you saw this," Weber called after her, as he shook his fist. He stalked back to the barn.

"He wanted that real bad," Phoebe said to Seth, once they stopped running and were safely on the other side of the block. "Do you think he's the one who really hit Hilary?"

"It's starting to look that way," Seth answered, as he stared back at the widow's walk of the Prescott house towering above the trees. "That would explain why he never noticed our scratch. The accident happened only a few days later, and he probably just assumed the scratch was part of the damage from it.

"And *I* had to drop the receipt," groaned Phoebe.

"Well, if you hadn't dropped it, Weber might have caught us."

"But what if he finds out who we are?" she said with a shudder. "He might come after us again. He knows we read that receipt."

73

"We'll have to be careful." Seth rubbed his throbbing temples with his fingers. "Do you remember the name of the body shop in Wilmington?"

"It started with a 'B', I think. I'm not sure."

"Some detectives we are," he muttered.

"Shouldn't we go to the police? If Weber is the one who hit Hilary, then Captain Van Arkle could arrest him before he destroys the receipt."

"He probably got rid of it already. Besides, Van Arkle isn't going to do anything just because we *claim* we saw a bill from an out-of-state repair shop whose name we can't remember. Weber will deny he ever had his car fixed. It'll be our word against his, and we're just a couple of kids." Seth shook his head. "Not to mention the half-dozen laws we broke going into that garage. We'll just get ourselves in trouble and it won't do Max any good anyway."

"But the scratch—"

"Who knows about that except us?" said Seth. "If we're going to help Max, we need proof that there *was* another car and that it was Weber's. And we better find it before Max pleads guilty."

"How are we going to get proof now that the receipt's gone?"

Seth shook his head and sighed. "I don't know."

Seth glanced at the clock above the door. The third person to give the "Quality of Mercy" speech from *The Merchant of Venice* had just finished. He figured it took about five minutes for each speech, including catcalls and applause. With nineteen minutes left in the period and four people ahead of him, he might

74

make it out of class without getting a zero, if his luck held.

"The quality of mercy is not strained," began Sandra Drury in a clear, confident voice. "It droppeth as the gentle rain from heaven."

He hated Shakespeare. He hated memorizing speeches. He hated sitting in last period english on a Friday, listening to thirty kids give the same speech over and over. And he hated having a last name that started with "F". If he had a "Y" name, he wouldn't have to bother memorizing. By the time Mrs. Besemer got to him, he'd know the speech by heart from hearing it so many times.

"Must needs give sentence against the merchant there." Sandra smiled triumphantly and took her seat. Definitely an A+.

Tom Engle sauntered to the front. He'd be good for at least six minutes, thought Seth. As usual, Mrs. Besemer would have to prompt him. He talked at half-speed even when he could remember what he was supposed to say.

The room was stifling. Every place his clothes touched him was damp with perspiration. Stretching his legs into the aisle, Seth pulled the denim away from his skin.

Outside, the sun was bright and warm—a gorgeous Indian summer day, perfect for shooting baskets at the parking lot hoop. But this afternoon Seth had other plans.

He had spent the previous night thinking about Max and the accident—which was why he hadn't gotten around to memorizing his speech. He was certain

75

Owen Weber's Mercedes had struck Hilary. Everything pointed to that conclusion. The scratch which disappeared during the week following the accident. The repair slip. That Weber lived only a block from the accident site. Even the fact that Max and Hilary remembered hearing the car. The Mercedes' diesel engine made quite a racket.

But Seth didn't think that would be enough for Captain Van Arkle, especially when he found out how they happened to see the repair slip.

"Seth Findeison, you're next," said Mrs. Besemer.

He looked up, surprised to hear his name already. "It's not my turn yet."

"It most certainly is." She crossed her arms like an Indian chief conducting a powwow. "And I hope you are better prepared than your two predecessors."

As Seth frantically tried to figure out where his calculations had gone wrong, the bell rang.

"Well, Mr. Findeison, it appears the gods have granted you a weekend for more practice." She tapped his desk with her knuckle. "I trust your speech will be that much better."

Thankful for the reprieve, Seth escaped into the hallway. His mouth felt as if he'd just eaten a bag full of salted nuts. He wanted to go home, lie next to his fan, and guzzle a liter of cold soda, but that would have to wait. He had to talk to Max first.

The apartment house was like an oven. The air was so humid and stuffy that Seth could hardly breathe. By the time he climbed the stairs to the second floor, his cotton shirt was soaked and his hair was wet with sweat.

Several minutes passed before Max answered his knock. He looked surprised to see Seth. "I hear that Hilary comes home tomorrow," the man said, as Seth entered the apartment.

"How did you know?" asked Seth.

"I check with the hospital every day. They told me."

Seth noticed that Max's cheeks were flushed and puffy. The black circles under his eyes made him look several years older than he had just a few days before.

"You call about Hilary every day?" he said.

Nodding, Max shuffled across the room to the kitchen area. "Hot as blazes. I'd offer you a cold drink, but this is all I have." He pulled a bottle of beer from the refrigerator.

"Water's fine," said Seth.

"So, what's up?" asked Max, as he filled a glass in the sink and dropped in three ice cubes.

An hour ago, Seth had planned to tell Max about Weber and the Mercedes. Together, he and Max could convince the police that the wrong man had been arrested.

Then, it had seemed like a great idea. But now, as Seth watched him, he began to have doubts. He wasn't sure what Max would do if he found out Owen Weber had been the other driver . . . especially since he was drinking again. If Max confronted Weber, there was no telling what might happen. Besides, Seth realized, the police were no more likely to believe Max and him than they were to believe him alone. Who was going to pay attention to a kid and a drunk?

"I thought you might like some company," said

Seth, deciding it was best for now to keep his information about the Mercedes to himself.

"Real considerate of you." Max handed the ice water to Seth, then twisted open his beer bottle. "But I told you last time not to worry about me."

"I've been thinking, Max," Seth began. "What if you could *prove* that another car hit Hilary?"

Max took a gulp of beer and sat down on one of the kitchen chairs. "We've been over this before, son. The police couldn't find any evidence of the other car. No skid marks. Nothing. They even ran an announcement in the newspaper asking the woman who called the ambulance to contact them. No dice there, either."

"But there's always a chance something will show up. You shouldn't give up yet." Seth pulled over the second chair for himself. "You always told us not to stop playing our hardest until the game was over."

Max stroked the neck of the beer bottle with his fingers. "I appreciate what you're trying to do for me, Seth. But I've done all I can to convince people I didn't hit your sister. I don't have any more shots to take." Closing his eyes, he leaned his head against the wall.

As he stared at his former coach, Seth felt his anger swelling inside. He was angry at the police for not believing Max, and at Weber for driving away from the accident and hiding what he did, and at Max for letting himself end up with a beer gut and no job.

Seth popped an ice cube into his mouth and crunched furiously until he calmed down.

After several minutes, Max opened his eyes. "If

you really want to do me a favor," he said, "how about changing the subject?"

Swallowing the last of the ice chips, Seth placed his glass on the table. "All right," he said, as he thought of the perfect topic. "Did I tell you about my new desk?"

"What desk was that?" asked Max.

"I needed a desk for homework, so I checked out the stuff on the curb the day they had that large item pickup. I found a beauty."

"Good for you." Max smiled, then took the last gulp of his beer. "More water?" he asked, as he reached into the refrigerator for another bottle.

"Okay," replied Seth, handing him his empty glass. "Guess where I found it? The Prescott house."

"Then it must be quality merchandise," said Max.

Seth waited until the man settled into his chair again. "What do you know about Owen Weber?"

Max's eyebrows rose. "Why the interest?"

"Do you know him?"

"Sure. I coached him when he was in high school." Max leaned back in his chair so it balanced on the rear legs. "Have a run-in with him?"

"A small one, when I got the desk."

"I figured," said Max. "Nobody who has anything to do with Owen goes long without running into trouble. The guy is poison. Always into something he shouldn't be."

"Like what?" asked Seth, eager to learn more about Weber.

"When he was a kid, it was drugs. His aunt always managed to keep most of that quiet. Of course, at school we knew what was going on." Max rubbed the gray stubble on his chin. "Lately, I've heard about him brawling at the bar down the street. Does some gambling, too. I'll tell you, if it hadn't been for Gertrude Prescott, Owen would've landed in the clink years ago."

Seth crunched his ice. "Gambling? Is that how he got the money for his Mercedes?"

"*His* Mercedes? No way. He doesn't have a dime. Never did an honest day's labor in his life. And he's a lousy gambler." Max shook his head. "No, that's Mrs. Prescott's car. He drives it, that's all."

"Only the two of them live in that big house?" asked Seth, remembering the woman's face he saw at the window the day he and Phoebe carted off the desk.

"Right. Owen is her younger brother's boy. He came to live with Mrs. Prescott when Chandler—that was her husband—took ill. Owen was supposed to help around the place. She kept him on when Mr. Prescott died." Max wiped his forehead with his handkerchief.

"Chandler D. Prescott," said Seth, thinking about the initials on his rolltop desk. "When did he die?"

"A few years back. Heart attack," replied Max, stuffing the dampened cloth into his pants pocket. "Sorry to see him go. He used to donate money for the summer Little League. As nice a guy as you'd ever want to meet." Max placed his empty bottle on the table. "Hey, why the curiosity about the Prescotts and Weber?"

"I told you," Seth said. "I got the desk from their place. I think it belonged to Chandler Prescott."

Max studied him for a moment. Then he reached across the table and grasped Seth's wrist. "Don't go getting yourself in trouble with Weber, just in case that's what you're planning on doing."

"Why would I do a stupid thing like that?" Seth replied, trying hard to sound sincere.

Max released his grip. "It *would* be stupid. And don't you forget it."

Hilary's homecoming the next day did not turn out to be the happy occasion they'd all been anticipating. While his parents went to pick her up, Seth spent the morning painting a watercolor of a daisy field to surprise her. He had just finished when he heard the car drive up.

"Aren't these flowers lovely?" said Mrs. Findeison, as she carried a large arrangement through the front door. "The girls at The Spot sent them to Hilary in the hospital."

Mr. Findeison followed her in, carrying Hilary to the sofa and propping her shoulders with throw pillows.

"How you doing, Hil?" said Seth, as he came into the living room.

"The itching under this leg cast is driving me crazy," she said. "I was better off in the hospital. At least it was air-conditioned."

"The warm spell is temporary, dear," Mrs. Findeison said patiently, opening the window near the sofa.

"You'll be more comfortable soon." Seth noticed the deep lines furrowed across his mother's forehead.

"Lighten up, Hilary," Seth said. "You're home and you're going to be as good as new in no time."

"I'll never be as good as new again," Hilary said, pointing to her bandaged forehead. "It's hideous. I'll never be able to model. I'll never be able to do anything. No one will want to look at me!"

"You can get plastic surgery," said Seth, trying to make her feel better.

"Oh sure. And who's going to pay for it? Your drunken coach?" She pointed to their father. "Or him? Not much chance."

Mr. Findeison turned and hurried upstairs.

"I'm sorry, Daddy," Hilary called after him. "I didn't mean it." She began to sob. "I don't want anyone to see my face."

Mrs. Findeison cradled Hilary in her arms. "It's all right. You don't have to see your friends yet."

"I *never* want anyone to see my face."

Seth thought of the watercolor sitting on his desk. A field of daisies wouldn't be enough to cheer Hilary, that was certain.

He had hoped that having her home would calm his parents and relieve the tension in the house. Now he realized that things would only get worse.

He had to get away. Slamming the front door behind him, he fled the house and sprinted down the street toward the far end of town. Even when his legs and lungs began to ache, he ran on, as though running hard and far enough might clear his mind. He didn't stop until he reached the abandoned train tracks near the river, where no one would bother him.

He knew it was too late to bring back the job he caused his father to lose. But at least he could help get the money for his sister's surgery from the man who caused her injuries. And the only way to do it was to convince the police that Owen Weber was that man.

Chapter 9

Seth didn't want to go home so soon. But after staring at the Schuylkill River's murky water for a couple hours, he realized the gnawing in his gut was caused by more than worry. He was hungry.

As soon as he opened the front door, he regretted coming back. "Where have you been?" Mrs. Findeison demanded. "I could have used your help this morning, what with Hilary coming home and everything."

"Help for what?" asked Seth.

"Never mind." She wiped her hands on her apron. "I took care of it myself."

"Sorry. It's just that she was so upset, I thought it was better if I left for a while." Seth followed her into the kitchen. "I'll get my own lunch and clean it up, too." Trying to stay out of his mother's way, Seth grabbed a handful of sliced ham and a hard roll.

"Miss Nichol called after you left," said Mrs. Findeison, reaching for the mayonnaise jar. "She was expecting you to move some boxes for her this morning. Now, Seth, if you promised—"

"I'll go right after I eat," he said, as he ducked out the back door. He found a shady spot under the pin oak to eat his lunch. The ham and dry roll, while satisfying his hunger, made him thirsty. But he had no intention of going back inside for a drink. His mother might find something else to bug him about.

Swallowing the last of his roll, he turned on the outside spigot next to the basement door and stuck his mouth under. The rusty taste made him gag. As he let the cool water run over his neck, the back screen door banged.

"Quite a scorcher, isn't it?" said his father from the porch. "In there, too." He motioned toward the kitchen. "Guess you needed some air, eh?"

"Yeah." Seth shook the water out of his hair.

"Want a sip?" Mr. Findeison leaned over the railing and handed him a can of cold soda.

Seth gulped down three mouthfuls. "Thanks."

"Finish it. I had one with lunch." He picked up Seth's basketball in the corner of the porch. "How about shooting a few with your old man? I think I'm still up to it."

Seth remembered the last time he had played with his father. It had been nearly half a year ago—right after the mill layoff. They'd gotten into an argument over the score. His dad had lost his temper and begun screaming. Mr. Gottshall had been painting his garage next door, and Seth had felt so embarrassed he'd wanted to run inside and hide. But his father wouldn't let him. They hadn't spoken to each other for days after that. From then on, Seth went over to the school to practice.

"Are you sure you want to, Dad?"

86

The man's jaw muscles tightened, and Seth knew his father remembered the last time, too.

"I'm sure," Mr. Findeison replied.

They stripped off their shirts and went over to the garage where the metal hoop was attached. It didn't take long for the game to start rolling. The pace was slower because Mr. Findeison had lost his quickness. But he made all his shots, so the score was close.

While they played, Mr. Findeison cracked jokes and teased with Seth. It was almost the way it used to be, and Seth wondered how he could have considered giving up the game. He loved it. They both did.

After fifteen minutes Mr. Findeison tossed Seth the ball and collapsed on the grass. "Time for a break," he said, breathing hard. "The body's not in such great shape anymore."

"You never used to shoot that good," said Seth.

"Once in a while I come out and practice. It helps me let off steam when things get rough." The creases at the corners of his mouth deepened slightly. "Lately, there have been days I've given that backboard a real pounding."

Seth rolled the ball back and forth on the grass between his outstretched legs. Hearing his dad talk about his feelings made him uncomfortable. It reminded him of how the layoff had changed everything.

Mr. Findeison wiped the sweat from his forehead. "Team tryouts coming up soon, aren't they?"

"End of next week." Why did his dad have to bring up the basketball team?

"You been practicing?"

87

"Some."

"I can't wait until the season starts." A broad smile spread across Mr. Findeison's face. "Seeing you dribbling that ball down the court . . ." He rubbed his hands up and down his arm. "Just the thought gives me tingles."

"I'm glad, Dad," Seth said automatically. He knew his father would be devastated if he didn't try out for the team. It wouldn't matter if he didn't make varsity. Junior varsity would be fine. He just wanted to see Seth playing. The roll Seth had had for lunch felt as if it had petrified inside his stomach.

"You make me proud, son. Real proud," Mr. Findeison continued. "Your mother pretends she doesn't care about it, but she feels the same way."

Proud. What a joke! Seth felt like laughing. Or crying. His father wouldn't be so proud if he knew the truth.

"School okay, then?"

"I got an A− on the last math quiz," Seth replied.

"Good. That's good," said his father. "Education is everything. That's where I went wrong."

Seth picked up the ball and dribbled toward the basket. "Come on, Dad. Let's play."

To Seth's relief, Mr. Findeison pushed himself up. "Okay, but watch out. I'm on a roll."

And he was. Layups, jumps, hook shots—he made them all. Seth hadn't seen his father so excited and happy for months.

But several minutes later Mrs. Findeison called from an upstairs window. "Would you two stop that racket? Hilary's trying to sleep."

The magic was broken.

For a short while, Seth had been able to forget about his lie, the mill layoff, the accident. He hated his mother and Hilary for ending that moment.

"Too bad we had to stop," said Mr. Findeison, as if he had shared the thought with Seth. "We'll play another time."

Seth pulled on his shirt. "I should go over to Miss Nichol's anyway. She's expecting me."

"About this morning . . . " began his father, reaching for his own shirt.

"I didn't know Mom had some chores for me."

His father shook his head. "Forget that. Look, the way you ran out . . . I know you were upset. I'm sorry for putting you through all this."

"Putting me through what?" said Seth, knowing that *he* should be the one apologizing.

"Me being out of work for so long. Then this situation with Hilary." He put his arm around Seth's shoulder. "We don't want you to worry about any of it. Just concentrate on your schoolwork and basketball tryouts. You'll do that for me, won't you?"

Seth felt a tightening in his throat, as though invisible fingers were clutching his neck. "It's not your fault, Dad," he said.

"I've really messed up," Mr. Findeison said.

"No, you haven't." Then, before his father could see his tears, Seth ran down the driveway into the street.

As Miss Nichol opened her door, the poodle sprang at Seth like a jack-in-the-box. He tried to shoo her away from his ankles, but as he swatted, the dog nipped his fingers.

"I don't understand why Babette acts so rudely around you, Seth. It's most peculiar." Scooping up the dog, Miss Nichol straightened the yellow bow in the center of Babette's curly head.

Seth noticed that the woman's white hair was uncombed and her dress wrinkled. "Should I have called first?" he asked.

"Oh, look at me," she chuckled, as she smoothed her dress. "I was resting on the couch."

"I can come back later."

"No, it was time to get up anyway. Babette will be wanting her afternoon walk." She closed the front door. "How silly of me to doze off in the middle of the day."

"I would have come earlier," said Seth, "but my sister got home from the hospital this morning."

"And how is she?" asked Miss Nichol.

"Better, I guess."

"I'm glad." She started up the staircase, beckoning for him to follow. Babette, with a wary eye on Seth, stayed close at the woman's heels. "I finished packing these last night," said Miss Nichol, entering her bedroom where half a dozen boxes were piled on the floor.

"Where do you want them?" asked Seth.

"These go to the attic, except for the ones with the 'L', which go downstairs." She touched the lid of the box with her foot. "Bring that along for the attic."

As Seth lifted the heavy box, he felt the strain in his arm and back muscles and knew the job would

90

give him more of a workout than an hour in the weight room. Somehow the physical effort seemed to lessen the dull ache in his head.

"The Friends of the Library called several weeks ago to see if I could donate any books to their annual sale," Miss Nichol continued, as she proceeded to the study at the end of the hall. "I thought it was an ideal time to weed through my collection."

Seth sat his box at the bottom of the attic steps and followed her into the study. "Where does this one go?" he asked, pointing to a box near his feet. "It's not marked."

"I thought Phoebe might want these." She leaned down and opened the flap of the box. "They're just some old family albums and poetry books. Phoebe loves poetry, you know. Young girls are quite romantic."

"I know," murmured Seth.

"You do?" Miss Nichol glanced at him from the corner of her eye.

"Because of my older sister," he said quickly. He knew his cheeks must be scarlet. He grabbed a book from the box to hide behind.

"That's my high school yearbook you have there," said Miss Nichol, gently tapping the binding. "Class of 1931. Depression years. But we had fun just the same. I was looking through it last night. Let me show you the photograph of my senior class picnic."

She plucked the book from Seth's hands. He was still blushing, but fortunately, Miss Nichol didn't seem to notice.

"Here it is." She held the page for him to see.

About thirty smiling young people stood by the shore of a lake. "There I am. I always stood in the back row."

Looking down at the frail woman beside him, Seth had a hard time imagining Miss Nichol as the tall, athletic-looking girl in the picture, although a check of the names beneath the photograph confirmed it.

But as he read the caption, his eye was drawn to another familiar name. "That guy next to you. Is he the same Chandler Prescott from the big house at Chestnut and Sixth?"

Miss Nichol sighed. "Yes. That was Chandler. A wonderful man."

"I have his desk in my room," said Seth.

"How in the world did you come to have Chandler's desk?"

"It was out on the curb on garbage day, and I took it home. I guess Mrs. Prescott didn't want it."

Miss Nichol clicked her tongue. "Sounds like something Gertrude would do. To take a family heirloom and send it to the dump, just because she was tired of it. She's never changed."

"You know her then?" asked Seth.

"I haven't spoken to her in decades. By choice, I might add." Miss Nichol jabbed her finger at the second row of the class photograph. "There she is. Gertrude Weber," she said disdainfully.

"That doesn't look anything like her," said Seth. "She looks so fat in that picture."

" 'Solid' would be a kinder term."

"And she's standing."

"The accident happened later." Miss Nichol shut the yearbook abruptly and placed it in the box.

"She was crippled in an accident?"

"You don't expect me to tell you about *that*, do you?" She settled into her chair by the desk, and Seth knew she intended to tell him whether he was interested or not.

"I've seen Mrs. Prescott around in her wheelchair," he said. "I wondered how—"

"It happened in July, after our graduation," Miss Nichol began. "Gertrude had gone to the Prescotts' to ride. She was always chasing Chandler—quite shamelessly, we all thought. In any case, she fell off one of the horses. She wasn't a very good rider, so it wasn't a surprise to anyone. But strangely, the Prescotts were very hush-hush about the entire incident."

"Did people ever find out what happened?" asked Seth.

"There was quite a bit of whispering at the time. But I always thought . . ." She shook her head. "I'm afraid it might have been Chandler's fault somehow. At least he must have thought so. It's the only way to explain the rest."

"The rest?"

"Chandler married Gertrude that autumn, even though he barely tolerated her before."

"Do you mean he married her because he thought the accident was his fault?" asked Seth.

Miss Nichol rose from her chair. "It's only my personal opinion, mind you. But it was just the sort of honorable gesture Chandler would have felt the situation demanded." She reached down for Babette.

93

"He was never the same after the accident. We all noticed the change. He became a sadder man."

Seth stared at her as the words penetrated. He had a good idea how Chandler Prescott might have felt, believing he was responsible for Gertrude's injuries. His temples began to throb again.

"Are you all right, Seth?" Miss Nichol said. "I think you need some air."

Despite his protests, she grasped his arm and led him downstairs.

"How inconsiderate of me to keep you stuck in that stuffy room while I rambled about ancient history."

"I'm okay, really, Miss Nichol," said Seth, as she sat him down in the kitchen.

"How about some freshly squeezed lemonade?"

"I'll finish moving the boxes." He pushed himself out of the chair.

"First you'll sit and have some lemonade." She placed a firm hand on his shoulder. "I insist."

Realizing he had no choice, Seth relaxed in the chair. Babette jumped into the seat across from him and fixed a warning gaze on him.

"That's better," Miss Nichol said, as she poured the lemonade into a tall yellow glass. "I'm sure you have enough on your mind these days without hearing about other people's hardships."

"No, it was interesting," he replied. The tartness of the lemonade puckered his lips.

"That's the real McCoy. Not one of those artificial concoctions." She sipped from her glass. "Just the right amount of sugar, don't you think?"

Seth nodded, although as far as he could tell, the lemonade had not a trace of sweetness.

Miss Nichol reached for a potted plant on the windowsill behind the sink. "I thought your sister might enjoy this African violet. It'll be in bloom soon. Nothing like flowers to cheer someone up, I always say."

"Thanks. I'm sure she'll like it."

"Let me give it a good soaking before you take it."

"I was wondering, Miss Nichol," said Seth, as she added water to the soil, "do you know Mrs. Prescott's nephew, too?"

"Owen? I'm afraid so. A gruesome person."

"Gruesome?" He didn't like her choice of words.

Suddenly, Babette jumped from the chair and ran to the door. "I forgot all about your walk, dear, didn't I?" said Miss Nichol, kneeling to pick up the yapping dog. She turned to Seth. "I better not keep her waiting any longer. Are you sure you feel better now? You looked rather pale before."

"I'll finish moving the books." He put his half-filled glass in the sink.

"Don't forget the violet when you go," she said, as she opened the back door.

After the woman left, Seth rested his elbow on the counter and rubbed his forehead with the tips of his fingers. Would the throbbing ever stop?

If only Hilary and Max had been nowhere near the corner of Sixth and Main that Tuesday morning when Owen Weber came barrelling through the intersection. If only he hadn't lied to his father. If only everything could be all right again.

Chapter 10

By the end of the weekend, the hot weather had passed. But things hadn't cooled off much at the Findeison house.

The Five Little Monsters returned bright and early Monday morning, and the final bit of peace and quiet in the house disappeared with their arrival. Whenever Seth was home, he had to dodge his mother running after a monster or his father carting things up and down the stairs for Hilary. And his sister, who refused to leave her room or let any of her friends visit, became even more irritable.

Seth decided to give them all a wide berth at the end of the day, barricading himself in his room where he could catch up on neglected homework assignments and avoid their short tempers.

The varsity basketball coach had announced that tryouts would begin Thursday. The first cut would be at the end of practice that day. Seth hadn't decided what to do about the team, but he practiced anyway, just in case. Besides, it gave him an excuse to stay away from the house.

Each day he stayed late at school, shooting baskets in the gym until the janitors chased him out. Once

Bryan, Lee, and Jon came in to play, but they left Seth alone. He preferred it that way.

At twilight on Tuesday as he headed home from the gym, Seth spotted Phoebe crossing Beech Street with her empty newspaper sack slung over her shoulder. He ran to catch up with her. When he tapped the back of her shoulder, she jumped.

"Oh it's you," she said, holding her hands to her chest. "You nearly gave me a heart attack sneaking up on me like that."

"I didn't think I'd scare you. Why are you so jittery?"

"Aren't you?" she said.

It wasn't like Phoebe to be nervous. "You mean about Weber?"

"Of course, I mean Weber," she snapped. "And where have you been? I called your house yesterday. Nobody even knew when you'd be home."

"I've been practicing in the gym." He touched her arm. "Have you seen Weber?"

Phoebe looked behind her toward the street. "He's been following me, Seth. I know it. I thought I saw him Saturday morning when I was doing my route, but I wasn't sure. Then yesterday his car passed me at least four times."

"It's probably a coincidence," he said, trying to be reassuring. But he, too, had noticed the silver Mercedes parked across from the school the previous morning.

"What do you think he's going to do?" She fingered the strap of her sack. "I'm scared, Seth."

"That's what he wants. He figures if we're scared, we won't say anything about the receipt."

"But what if he's planning more than that? Let's go to the police."

"How can we do that, Phoebe? Without the receipt, we don't have any proof that Weber hit Hilary. Besides, we broke into his garage. You can get in really big trouble for something like that."

"If we knew the name of the repair shop, then the police would know we were telling the truth, and they'd overlook the breaking-in part."

"You know we aren't going to remember it," said Seth.

"I can't stand this." Her voice was panicky.

"Weber won't do anything," Seth said, "because he knows if he did, we'd go right to the police."

"Is that supposed to make me feel better?"

He put his arm around her shoulder. "I'm not worried about Weber. You shouldn't be either." He hoped he was right in what he said.

He felt her body relax a bit. "I should be thinking of ways to help Max, instead of imagining the worst about Weber," said Phoebe.

But Seth saw she was still uncomfortable, so he offered to walk her home. She didn't talk much while they walked, and when they reached her house, she scurried inside like a frightened mouse.

Seth wished he had never let Phoebe get involved in the entire mess.

On Wednesday afternoon, Hilary was scheduled for a checkup at the hospital. Mrs. Findeison couldn't go because of the Five Monsters, so Mr. Findeison asked Seth to come along and help lift Hilary in and out of the car.

When they arrived at the hospital, Seth stayed in the lobby downstairs while his father took Hilary up to see the doctor. Watching the patients pass by, he wondered what brought them there. He could almost guess by studying the faces of family members. The sadder the eyes, the worse the illness. Strangely, it made him feel better about his sister. As bad as her injuries were, at least she had a future. But he knew that she didn't see it that way.

"Excuse me," said the woman beside him. "Do you have the time? The clock on the wall must be broken."

"Quarter to five," he replied.

"My husband's therapy is taking longer than usual today. Have you been waiting long?"

"About forty-five minutes."

"Is it a relative?" she asked.

"What?"

"Or is it a friend you're waiting for?"

Seth was taken aback by her nosiness. Then he realized she was trying to make conversation. "My sister."

"I hope it's nothing serious."

"She was in a car accident a few weeks ago."

The woman smiled knowingly. "Things like that can be difficult for the family, can't they?"

"Was your husband in an accident, too?"

"Not exactly. He lost both legs in Vietnam."

Seth regretted asking. "I'm sorry."

"Don't be embarrassed. He manages quite well."

"Oh." Seth didn't know what to say after that.

"We just came back from a trip to Canada. Would you like to see the snapshots? I picked them up on our way over here."

Before he knew it, she pulled a bulging envelope from her purse. She had a long, detailed story for each shot. After the fiftieth scenic view of shimmering lakes and snow-capped mountains, Seth decided he'd seen as much of Canada as he would ever want to.

Finally, she showed him a photograph of a man in sunglasses and a Phillies cap, sitting in the driver's seat of a white Oldsmobile. A U.S. Customs sign hung on the building in the background.

"This is Tom at the border. We were stuck there twenty-five minutes because of all the shopping we'd done." She laughed. "But it was worth the wait."

"Your husband drives?" Seth asked.

"Oh yes." Seeing his puzzled expression, she added, "We have manual controls on the steering wheel for the brake and gas."

"I didn't know you could get gadgets like that."

"It's made all the difference for Tom," she said. "He always loved driving."

His father's voice across the lobby caught Seth's attention. "Guess they're finished," he said to the woman. He waved goodbye and walked over to meet his family.

He saw immediately that the visit hadn't gone well. Some of Hilary's bandages had been removed, and she tried to hide her face with her hands. His father looked as if he'd just watched the Eagles lose a close one by a field goal in the final twenty seconds.

"I wish you'd consider my suggestion, Mr. Findeison," said the doctor, a young man with wire-rim glasses. "Our counseling services are done on a sliding-scale basis, so the cost shouldn't affect your decision."

"We've been through this before." Seth's father was annoyed.

"And I'll repeat what I told you," said the doctor. "It will help all of you."

"Let's go, Seth," Mr. Findeison said, pushing open the glass door and wheeling Hilary outside.

On the way home, Hilary stared out the rear window, refusing to speak. "What was the doctor talking about?" Seth asked his dad.

"Nothing," Mr. Findeison said. "And don't mention it to your mother."

"But—"

"I don't want to hear any more about it."

They drove the rest of the way in silence.

When they arrived home, Seth planned to duck into his room before anyone thought of a reason to yell at him. But as soon as he opened the front door, he was caught in the crossfire.

"How did it go?" Mrs. Findeison stood at the dining room table, diapering the Shin-kicker.

"Take a look," said Seth, holding the door for his father, who carried Hilary.

"Oh!" said Mrs. Findeison as she saw Hilary's face. Unable to hide her shock, she covered her mouth with her hand. "They took some bandages off."

"I'm beautiful, aren't I?" cried Hilary, making her first sound since leaving the hospital.

"Boo!" the Shin-kicker called, as Mrs. Findeison lowered him to the floor.

"Oh shut up!" screamed Hilary.

"I'll take her up," mumbled Mr. Findeison, as he awkwardly maneuvered Hilary and her leg cast up the stairs.

"What did the doctor say?" Mrs. Findeison demanded of Seth.

"Don't ask me. I just sat in the lobby," he replied, keeping a wary eye on Shin-kicker.

"Your father might not tell me everything. You know how he's been about this."

"Sorry, Mom."

"The scars don't look *that* bad, do they, Seth?" she asked. "Oh poor Hilary."

The Whiner tugged at Mrs. Findeison's elbow. "When will my mommy be here?"

"Soon, Kimmi."

"I'm going to my room," said Seth, stepping over the Sneak, who sat on the bottom stair. Just as he reached the second floor, the Human Wrecking Ball come barreling down the hall like a runaway locomotive. The child swerved around Seth and slid down the staircase on his stomach. Seth raced to his room and threw open the door.

He felt sick.

The top of his desk was rolled open and the contents of every drawer and compartment were spewed across the floor. Pens were scattered on his bed and chair. His best drawing paper, spread across his desk, was decorated with scribbles and lines. A bottle of ink lay on its side, dripping black liquid onto the floor.

Lifting the paper, he discovered several nibs. Then, to his horror, he noticed the indentations in the wood. T-R-E-V-O-R.

"Mom!" He charged down the hall, descending the stairs in three bounds. "Where is that brat?"

The Human Wrecking Ball clutched Mrs. Findeison's leg. Seth grabbed his arm.

"Seth!" she exclaimed. "What are you doing?"

"He ruined my desk! Engraved his name in it, spilled ink. My room's a disaster."

"Trevor, is that so?" Mrs. Findeison said.

"Jeremy made me."

"Did not!" the Sneak retorted.

"I should have known." Seth yanked the Sneak to his feet. "What's in your hand?"

"Nothing."

He reached behind the four-year-old's back. "It's one of my pens. You little-ouch!" Pain shot through his left leg. Shin-kicker took two more shots with his Oxfords before Mrs. Findeison pulled the boy off.

"Uh-oh," yelled the Screamer. "Kimmi went pee-pee."

The Whiner stood in a yellow puddle, clutching her blankie.

"What next?" Throwing up her hands, Mrs. Findeison ran to the kitchen for a towel.

The three boys, their attention diverted from Seth to something much more interesting, gathered around the crying girl. Their taunts made her sob even louder.

"Mother!" Hilary's voice from above cut through the clamor. "Can't you shut them up? They're giving me a headache."

"I'll be there in a minute," Mrs. Findeison called to her, as she blotted the soaked carpet.

Mr. Findeison came downstairs and gaped at the scene. "I told you I didn't want them in my house anymore."

He was drowned out by the high-pitched shrieks of the monsters. The Whiner swung at the jeering boys with her fist. One of them shoved her.

"Stop it, all of you!" his mother screamed.

Seth brought her another towel from the kitchen.

"I'm sorry about your desk," she said to him. "I'll help you clean it up later."

"Never mind," he replied, feeling sorry for her. "I'll get Hilary an aspirin." He brushed by his father and hurried upstairs again.

By the time he returned to his room, the roar downstairs had subsided. His mother managed to quiet the monsters, and his father retreated to his bedroom and turned on the television.

Seth sunk into his desk chair and surveyed the mess. He rubbed his palm over the letters carved into the once-smooth mahogany surface. Fortunately, the wood was hard and the marks weren't too deep. He'd planned on refinishing the desk anyway. He wasn't as upset as he might have been if it had happened another time. Right now all he could think about was his parents.

105

At that moment, he made his decision about the basketball team. Seeing his parents just then—distressed, overwhelmed, almost helpless—convinced him that he had only one choice. It would disappoint them too much if he didn't make the team. The way things were going, they might not have much to celebrate for a long time.

He'd try out and make varsity. He had to. For them.

Chapter 11

"I didn't know if you'd show or not." Bryan swung his leg over the locker room bench and sat down beside Seth.

"I showed. You happy now?" Seth said, as he tightened the laces on his shoes.

"You're not still burned up about that business with Max, are you?"

"I've got a lot on my mind." Seth kicked his locker door shut and tucked his shirttail into his shorts.

"Every guy in this room has a lot on his mind," said Bryan, following him into the gym. "Hey, I hear there's this new kid trying out who shoots sixty percent from the free throw line."

Seth knew that Bry wanted to make peace, but he didn't care. "I don't want to talk now," he said curtly, and he strode across the floor.

He needed the few moments before the coach came out to fix his mind and body on basketball. He'd been playing mental games all day, focusing on the hoop and imagining himself sinking every shot. He knew that if he allowed thoughts of Weber, Max, Hilary, or especially his father to interrupt his concentration, his performance would suffer.

107

When the coach arrived, he directed the boys to sit on the bleachers. Then he gave the standard speech about how he wished he had the money to suit up everyone who showed. But what he really wanted, thought Seth, was a handful of guys who were good enough to get him another league championship. As far as the coach was concerned, the rest of them could play intramurals.

There were about thirty guys, half eighth-graders, and everybody was nervous. Except for Lee. He looked as cool as the varsity players who leaned against the opposite wall sizing up the group on the bleachers.

Lee turned his head and caught Seth watching him. He smirked, then looked away. It gave Seth another reason to make the team.

As they climbed off the bleachers onto the court and grabbed balls, Seth surveyed the competition. He figured he had a chance to be one of those chosen for varsity—at least to make the first cut—if he could keep his mind on his game.

It started going wrong during the first drill. His passes were wide. The ball skipped off his fingertips. His timing was flawed. He tried to fight it, tried to stop the memory from blocking his concentration, but it was no use.

He kept remembering the night he lied about the call from the mill and how they'd driven to Philadelphia and how the 76ers had won and they'd all celebrated—except for Seth. The lie wouldn't release him. He was its prisoner.

He made less than fifty percent of the layups and

108

lost the ball every time in the dribbling drill. He'd blown it, he knew, even before they divided up to play a game. Still, he hoped if he could get it right then—show what he could do—maybe he had a chance.

He pushed himself, running hard and playing aggressively. But he fouled, double dribbled, made errors he'd stopped doing in sixth grade. When the coach pulled him out, Seth caught a glimpse of Bryan shaking his head. He wished it would end soon and he could get away from all of them.

At last the coach blew the whistle. Sweating and breathing hard, Seth dragged himself to the bleachers and collapsed on the bottom bench.

"Good going, Findeison," sneered Lee, as he stepped over Seth.

"Lay off," he said. If he had more energy, he would have grabbed Lee's ankle and thrown him to the floor.

The coach huddled with his assistant a final time, then flipped the sheet on his clipboard. Seth rested his chin in his hands and stared at the planking in the floor. He didn't want anyone to see his eyes in case he couldn't control his disappointment.

"I cut to fifteen today. Those left will practice Monday and Tuesday. Then I make the final." The coach cleared his throat and a stillness engulfed the group on the bleachers.

Seth felt no exciting anticipation. It had ended for him out on the court. He tried not to hear the names or shouts of relief, but couldn't ignore the ache in his gut when he heard that Bryan, Jon, and Lee had made the cut.

He nearly missed his own name, read last as if it had been an afterthought. He glanced up at the coach, surprised and not understanding.

The other guys crawled around him on their way to the locker room. The coach approached the bench and looked down at Seth.

"I didn't do that because I'm a nice guy, Findeison," he said. "I know you've got some problems at home. I don't give a damn about that." The coach leaned close to Seth's face. He smelled of cigarettes. "I watched you last year. I know what you could do for my team. That's all that saved you today, Findeison. Your potential." He clamped his hand on Seth's shoulder. "But potential alone isn't worth zip. You got that?"

Seth nodded.

"Pull yourself together by Tuesday or you won't even be playing jayvee."

Seth hurried to the locker room, his spirits lifted little by the coach's words. Although he was grateful for another chance, he knew things wouldn't be any different on Tuesday. What made him clutch today would happen again. It would have been better if the coach had cut him right off.

He showered and dressed quickly, making perfunctory replies to the few congratulations he received. Most of the guys probably thought he didn't deserve to make the cut.

Avoiding Bryan, Jon, and Lee, who were whooping

it up in the back row of lockers, Seth stuffed his gear in his nylon bag and headed out.

He felt like talking to Phoebe. She'd listen to what happened without plying him with questions he didn't want to answer. She'd be doing her newspapers somewhere west of Main Street. He wondered if he could find her. Turning at Seventh Avenue, Seth made his way in that direction.

He was too tired from the drills to hurry. Besides, he was in no rush. Phoebe didn't finish her route until six, and he didn't want to get home too soon.

If he timed it right—closer to dinner when the house was most hectic with mothers picking up their monsters, and Hilary crabbing about being hungry, and his dad engrossed in the local news—he might avoid a lengthy interrogation about the tryout.

The attack caught him completely off-guard. As Seth stepped from the curb at Chestnut Street, the silver Mercedes swerved around the corner, stopping directly in his path. Before Seth could react, Weber had jumped from the driver's seat and grabbed his arm.

"Let me go!" shouted Seth, as he tried to pull away from Weber's grasp.

"If you say a word about anything you saw in my car, some real rotten things are going to start happening."

"I don't know what you're talking about," said Seth.

"I know who you are," Weber growled, as he pressed Seth against the side of the car. The corner of his mouth twitched. "And I know who your little

111

girlfriend is, too. I know a lot about her. Like what she does after school and where I can find her if I want to.''

A wave of panic swept over Seth as Weber spoke. Phoebe had been right. They should have gone to the police. He pushed against Weber's massive chest with his shoulder. ''She doesn't have anything to do with it.''

Weber slammed him back against the car and pinned him there with his body. Seth felt his hot breath on his cheek. ''Be smart, kid. Don't make a scene.''

Twisting and shoving, Seth tried to untangle his arms and maneuver one of his legs behind Weber's.

''If you won't stand and talk nice,'' Weber hissed, ''maybe you'll have to take a little ride with me.''

As the man shifted his body to open the car door, Seth freed one of his pinned arms. He still held the nylon gym bag. Swinging his arm back, he flung the bag toward Weber's head. Instead, he hit the shoulder, but it was enough to surprise Weber. In the second that the man turned to his side, Seth twisted out from under his bulky frame and ran.

But *where* to run? He couldn't go to a stranger's house. Weber would collar him before anyone answered the doorbell. Phoebe's father would be home by now. Weber wouldn't mess with him. But her house was over three blocks away, his own even further. Seth was afraid Weber would catch him in a straight-out race to Phoebe's, since his legs were worn out from tryouts.

112

Making a quick decision, he turned in the opposite direction, back across Chestnut Street. He had occasionally mowed the Lichensteins' lawn on Main Street. If only he could make it there before Weber caught him.

Figuring he had a better chance cutting through familiar backyards than outrunning Weber on the street, Seth headed through the side yard of the corner house. He heard Weber close behind, shouting for him to stop. Seth weaved his way around bushes into the adjoining yard. Weber was gaining on him.

Seth ran between a garage and hedge, pausing to push two garbage cans across the narrow passageway. His gym bag snagged on one of the cans, but he couldn't risk stopping to get it loose.

One more house and he'd be at the Lichensteins'. He was winded and he had a cramp in his side. He cursed Weber's timing. If he hadn't just killed himself at basketball practice for three hours, he could have easily outrun the man. As it was, he was losing his small lead.

As Seth rounded the corner of the garage, he was alarmed to see that neither of the Lichensteins' two cars was there, meaning the house was probably empty. Weber was only about a hundred feet behind.

Then he remembered the fence. One day the previous summer when he was mowing, he had discovered a loose board in the wood plank fence. The neighborhood kids had been using it to get from yard to yard. The opening was narrow, but Seth thought he could squeeze through. Weber, however, would have to circle out to the street to get around the fence, giving Seth several more precious minutes.

"Give it up, Findeison. You don't have a chance," called Weber, entering the opposite side of the Lichensteins' yard.

Not bothering to look back, Seth raced for the loose board. Which one was it? He pushed on several, but none budged. It had been right next to the rhododendron, he was sure. Mr. Lichenstein must have nailed it shut.

Seth could hear Weber stomping across the yard toward him. He tried to suppress his panic. Frantically, he searched the fence for a way over. He knew he couldn't scale it. The fence was over seven feet high and there were no footholds. Not only that, but the top edges of the fence board were cut into sharp points, making it impossible to get a good grip.

Then he noticed a tree next to the fence a few feet away. If he could jump high enough to grab a branch, he might be able to swing over.

Taking a deep breath, Seth ran toward the tree and leaped for the branch nearest the fence. But his fingertips only brushed it.

He could hear Weber's labored breathing coming nearer. With no time for another running leap, Seth stood beneath the branch and jumped again. Higher this time, but not good enough to grasp the branch.

Pretend you're going for a rebound, thought Seth. Jump as though the game depended on it. "Got it!" he cried, wrapping his fingers around the branch and pulling his body up.

The next moment Weber was under him, trying to

grab his feet. Kicking his legs toward the top of the fence, Seth swung himself over. By the time he saw the brick chimney of the neighbor's barbecue on the opposite side of the fence, his legs had already scraped against its rough edges. He landed on top of the metal grill, bumping his head on the brick side as he fell.

He glanced down at his ripped jeans, then felt the warm trickle of blood on his cheek. Ignoring the oozing cuts on his leg and temple, he picked himself up.

Weber shouted an obscenity and pounded on the fence before he hurried away.

The detour over the fence had only gained Seth a few minutes, and he couldn't run much farther. He'd never make it to Phoebe's house. He had to find a safe place to hide. Miss Nichol lived two houses away, but he didn't want to involve her. She was a frail old woman, and Weber was . . . gruesome. She had used that word herself.

He glanced between the trees toward the street and spotted Weber coming around the end of the fence. With no other choice and no time to think, Seth summoned up the last of his strength and sprinted toward Miss Nichol's house. He knew the front door would be unlocked. He climbed the porch steps two at a time. Without knocking, he burst inside, slamming the door behind him.

Babette was on him within seconds, yapping and nipping at his heels.

Miss Nichol entered the hallway from the kitchen. "What's the meaning of this?" she demanded.

Weber pounded on the front door. "Open up! The kid's got something of mine and I want it."

"Please, Miss Nichol," cried Seth. "Don't let him in!"

Chapter 12

Miss Nichol stopped near the foot of the staircase. "Who's out there?" she asked Seth.

Before he could reply, the door burst open. Seth rammed his body against the wood, struggling to close the door. His effort had little effect on Weber, who forced himself halfway inside the house.

Then, to Seth's amazement, Babette clamped her jaws on Weber's leg. The man cried out and retreated to the porch. The poodle followed, still holding on.

Seth slammed the door and locked it.

"Get him off me!" cried Weber from outside.

"She'll let go when you get off my porch," Miss Nichol called to Weber through the closed door.

"Okay, okay," he said.

Seth pushed aside the heavy drape at one of the front windows and peered out. Weber had backed down to the sidewalk, kept at bay by Babette, who darted between his legs snapping at him.

"Call off the dog and open up, Miss Nichol," Weber shouted. "The kid took something that didn't belong to him."

Miss Nichol cracked the door a few inches. Seth

looked at her anxiously. "Go away, Owen," she said, "or I'll call the police."

"You're going to be sorry you said that," he replied. "I'll be back."

Babette stood in the center of the sidewalk, barking steadily until Weber was gone. Once the man was out of view, Miss Nichol opened the front door and the dog scampered in.

Kneeling down, Seth patted the poodle's curly head. "Thanks, Babette." The dog wagged her tail. "And thank you, Miss Nichol, for not letting him in."

"A despicable man," she muttered, shaking her head. She pointed to Seth's cheek. "Did he do that?"

"That and a lot more," Seth said, looking around the room. "Where's your phone?"

"In the kitchen. Who are you going to call?"

"The police." Seth hurried down the hall toward the back of the house.

"Is that necessary?" Miss Nichol followed him into the kitchen. "I'm sure he won't return."

"Maybe not here. But he threatened me and I don't think he was kidding around," he said, as he dialed the phone.

"What is this all about, Seth?"

"I found out that Weber was the one who hit Hilary, at least I thought there was a good chance. After what just happened, I'm positive of it."

"Oh my, you'd better make that call."

When the police dispatcher answered, Seth reported the assault. "They said an officer will be right over," he told Miss Nichol as he hung up.

"Come, let me clean off your face," she said, rinsing a cloth in the sink.

"I can't." He hurried to the back door. "I have to find Phoebe."

"What does Phoebe have to do with this?" she asked, frowning.

"She was with me when . . . it's a long story, but Weber might go after her the way he did me."

As he reached for the doorknob, the back door flew open, nearly smacking him in the face. Both Seth and Miss Nichol gasped.

It was Phoebe. "What's going on?" she asked.

Miss Nichol threw her arms around her niece, pulled her into the house, then locked the door. "Are you all right, dear?"

"I saw Owen Weber chasing Seth across Sixth Avenue," she replied. She turned to Seth. "I figured maybe you'd come here. What happened?"

"I just called the police," said Seth.

"I knew this was going to happen." Phoebe tossed her half-full newspaper sack on the floor by the refrigerator. "I told you we should have gone to the police. Oh you're bleeding!"

"Let me tend to that," said Miss Nichol, collecting her cloth and bandages from the counter. "And while I do, you two had better tell me why you're so sure Owen Weber was the guilty driver."

As she washed the blood off Seth's face and knee, he and Phoebe told of the disappearing scratch on the Mercedes and how they later saw the repair receipt from the body shop.

"Why didn't you go to the police, or at least to
119

your parents, with that information?'' asked Miss Nichol, as she taped a bandage to Seth's knee.

Seth and Phoebe exchanged looks. ''We might as well tell now,'' said Phoebe. ''The police are going to ask the same thing.''

''We were afraid we'd get into trouble. We found the receipt in Mrs. Prescott's barn. We broke in,'' said Seth. ''But it was my idea. Phoebe was only trying to help me.''

''I see.'' Miss Nichol gathered up her first aid equipment. ''And is that why you asked me about Owen the other day, Seth?''

''I only wanted to help Max. It isn't right that . . . ''

He was interrupted by the doorbell. Babette sprung from her perch on the kitchen chair and raced into the front hallway.

''That must be the police,'' said Seth. ''I'll go.''

Miss Nichol and Phoebe followed him into the hallway, and Miss Nichol scooped up the snarling Babette. None of them expected what they saw when Seth opened the door.

''Gertrude!'' Miss Nichol cried.

It was too late for Seth to close the door. Owen Weber had already pushed Mrs. Prescott's wheelchair inside. Seth stepped away from Weber, closer to Phoebe. The man had the advantage. Even Babette couldn't stop him now that he was inside the door.

''Hello, Amelia.'' Mrs. Prescott offered her hand. Miss Nichol kept her arms firmly wrapped around the poodle.

"I see it hasn't changed between us," Mrs. Prescott said, removing her black leather gloves.

"What do you want here?" Miss Nichol said coldly.

"I'm sorry to bother you, Amelia. When Owen told me what happened, I was afraid he might have been rude to you."

"No ruder than you."

"I came to apologize in case . . . well, you know how crass Owen can be. Sometimes people misunderstand his intentions." She paused, staring at Seth and Phoebe. "I think we can settle this problem quietly now."

Seth hadn't been sure why Weber had returned with Mrs. Prescott nor what the meaning of her actions was. But the way she looked at him convinced him that her words, though polite, were as threatening as Weber's.

Babette's growls became louder, and Seth heard footsteps on the porch. Praying that it was the police, he circled around Weber and pulled open the door.

Captain Van Arkle stood on the porch. "You were expecting me?" he said, peering at the group in the entryway.

As Van Arkle entered the house, Seth noticed a shocked expression on Mrs. Prescott's face. But it was fleeting. "I'm pleased you responded so promptly to my call, Captain," she said.

"But I'm the one who—" Seth began, but she cut him off.

"Actually, it was Owen who called. Wasn't it, Owen?"

Weber looked confused. "Uh, yeah."

121

"The dispatcher said there was an assault," said Van Arkle.

"No, no," said Mrs. Prescott. "A theft. Owen happened to recognize the thief on the street and followed him here. We called immediately."

Seth couldn't believe how she had turned everything around. "No, that's not it," he protested.

"He's the one, isn't he, Owen?" said Mrs. Prescott, pointing at Seth.

"That's him all right," said Weber.

Miss Nichol stepped toward Captain Van Arkle. "There's been a mistake. It was Seth who made the call from my kitchen. I heard it myself. Owen had chased him here."

"I'm shocked, Amelia!" exclaimed Mrs. Prescott. "I can't believe you had anything to do with this. To think you would lie about such a thing!"

"You are as contemptible as your nephew," said Miss Nichol.

Van Arkle held up his hands. "Hold it. I want some answers. Mrs. Prescott, exactly what was stolen and how do you know the Findeison boy was the thief?"

Mrs. Prescott raised her chin. "A valuable antique desk was removed from my barn," she said. "Owen later found this young man in the barn, apparently attempting to steal other things. The boy got away, and we didn't know who he was. Then this afternoon, Owen spotted him near the house and followed him here."

"That's a lie!" shouted Seth.

"Check his house," said Weber, glaring at Seth. "He's got that desk."

122

"We can do that," Van Arkle said.

"Sure, I've got the desk," Seth said. "But they set it out for garbage, and he told me I could have it."

"It's true. I was with him," said Phoebe.

"So you didn't break into their barn?" asked Van Arkle.

"Do you expect him to tell the truth?" said Mrs. Prescott.

"Let him talk," Van Arkle said.

"Okay, I broke into the barn. But it wasn't to steal anything. I wanted to look at the Mercedes."

Van Arkle frowned. Seth knew it was coming out all wrong. "When we were hauling away the desk," he said, trying to explain better, "it scraped the car. A few days later I noticed that the scratch was gone, and I couldn't figure out what happened."

"That's when we found the repair receipt from Delaware," said Phoebe. "And Weber chased us with a pitchfork and got the receipt back."

Weber glared at Seth and Phoebe.

"Max Hampton didn't hit my sister. It was the Mercedes," Seth went on. "Why else would Weber want to make sure I kept quiet about that receipt?"

"None of this makes much sense," said Van Arkle, shaking his head.

"The receipt showed work on the entire front side, including a replaced headlight and paint job," said Seth. "The car had been in an accident after the desk scratched it. And Weber took it out of state to be fixed."

Weber glanced nervously at his aunt.

"This is an outrageous accusation," said Mrs. Prescott. "He's obviously making up this story to protect himself."

Van Arkle turned to Seth and Phoebe. "If you had this information, why didn't you tell me before?"

"I didn't have any proof to show you, so we figured you wouldn't believe us."

"If you could find the repair shop in Wilmington," said Phoebe, "you'd know we're telling the truth. Someone down there is sure to remember the car."

Van Arkle took a notebook from his pocket. "I can check that out."

Weber stepped toward Seth. "You kids are full of—"

"That's enough, Owen," said Mrs. Prescott sharply. She turned to Captain Van Arkle. "Am I to assume that you believe the lies these children are telling and doubt my word about the theft of the desk?" Her voice was icy.

"I only said I'd check it out, Mrs. Prescott. That's what I'm paid to do."

"Phoebe and Seth are not ones to make up wild stories," Miss Nichol said. "I think, Captain, that you will find truth in what they say. I saw Weber pursue Seth with an obviously malevolent intent. I'm sure if you ask several of the neighbors, they can confirm that."

"I'll do that, Miss Nichol," he replied. "In the meantime, Owen, maybe you'd better come down to my office so we can chat with your probation officer about this assault business."

"Hey, hold on!" Weber backed away from his

aunt's wheelchair. "I didn't assault anybody. I was only trying to scare the kids. She made me."

"Calm down, Owen." Mrs. Prescott reached for his arm.

He yanked it away. "Nobody's going to pin this on me."

"Captain," said Mrs. Prescott, "you know Owen sometimes gets more . . . well, more physical than he should, especially when he drinks."

"I see what you're doing, Gertrude." Weber shook his fist at her. "You said I wouldn't have any trouble. I'm not taking the heat for this."

Mrs. Prescott's lips tightened and her eyes widened. "Stop it, Owen, before you—"

"It was her. She ran down that girl!"

Seth glanced at Phoebe. She grabbed his hand. For a moment, the room was absolutely silent. Everyone stared at Mrs. Prescott.

She sighed and shook her head. "I must apologize to all of you. I guess there's more to this than I knew." She looked at Van Arkle. "Perhaps there was a problem with the car, and Owen didn't tell me. I'd been in New York for two weeks and it may have happened in my absence. I assure you, Captain, I'll get to the bottom of this. Owen will accept responsibility for anything he's done."

"It was her. She *was* here. She was driving to the airport. She made me take the car to Wilmington that day so no one would know."

Van Arkle had out his notebook again. "Now when was it you said you left for New York, Mrs. Prescott?"

"Labor Day. You can call my friends there if you like."

Seth looked at Weber standing by the door. A stream of sweat ran down the man's reddened face. He didn't look so menacing anymore. Seth felt sorry for him, then realized why. He knew Weber was telling the truth.

"She's lying," Seth announced. "Mrs. Prescott couldn't have been in New York for two weeks starting on Labor Day. I saw her face in the window of her house the Saturday between Labor Day and the accident. Remember, Phoebe? The day we found the desk."

"You're right," said Phoebe. "I'd forgotten."

"I can't believe you'd listen to this, Captain Van Arkle," said Mrs. Prescott.

"It will be easy enough to check out airline reservations," said Van Arkle. "Then we'll see who's telling the lies."

"You'll hear from my lawyer," said Mrs. Prescott, pulling on her gloves.

"I'm used to that, Mrs. Prescott," he replied, as he opened the front door.

"Owen, get me out of here," she demanded.

"Get out yourself." Weber stalked out.

"I'll have more questions for you," Van Arkle said to Seth and Phoebe. "This better be on the level or you'll be in big trouble."

Miss Nichol placed an arm around both their shoulders as they watched Van Arkle wheel Mrs. Prescott out. "I told you justice would prevail," she said.

126

"It's not over yet," said Phoebe.

"It will be soon," said her aunt. "Captain Van Arkle believed what you said. And I could see in Gertrude's eyes that she was guilty as charged."

"You could see that?" said Seth. "She seemed so calm and in control. The way she twisted everything around was incredible."

"That's Gertrude." Miss Nichol stooped to pick up Babette.

"But how could Mrs. Prescott have been driving?" said Phoebe. "Her legs are paralyzed."

"Manual controls," Seth replied. "They're installed in cars for people who can't use foot pedals. I never heard of them until a woman in the hospital mentioned them. Remember how I caught my shoulder on that lever attached to the Mercedes' steering wheel? That's what it was."

"Would you two care for some tea?" asked Miss Nichol. "After all that excitement, I need a little."

"Oh no! I almost forgot my papers," said Phoebe. "I'd better go, Auntie. The subscribers hate their papers late."

"I'll help you," said Seth.

They left Miss Nichol sitting in her rocker, while Babette lay on the floor chewing a dog biscuit.

"With everything happening, you never told me how you did in tryouts," Phoebe said when they were outside.

"Not great," he muttered.

"Did you make the cut?"

He nodded.

She stopped and gently touched his arm. "Something's wrong. I thought it was because of the accident, but it's more than that, isn't it?''

''A lot more.'' He looked at her, wishing he could tell her, hoping that would make it go away, yet knowing it wouldn't. ''I'm not going to make the team, Phoebe.''

''Whatever it is, you can do *something*,'' she said.

''You don't understand.''

''I understand that you were probably the only person who didn't give up on Max Hampton—including Max. And if it wasn't for you, no one would have ever known about Mrs. Prescott. Don't give up on *yourself*.''

She was right. He had given up on himself. There *was* something he could do, and the time had come to do it.

Chapter 13

Seth planned to talk to his father immediately. But by the time he arrived home that evening, Captain Van Arkle had already called to tell the Findeisons about the new developments in the investigation. Seth spent the night filling in his family on the story and having his mother fuss over his cuts and bruises.

When he came home from school the next afternoon, Seth found an unexpected guest sitting on the living room sofa.

"Don't stand there with your mouth hanging open," said Mr. Findeison. "Come in here. We've been waiting for you."

Max was wearing a white shirt and tie and a smile that Seth remembered from his coaching days. He and Mr. Findeison were drinking coffee.

"Max has been telling me how you visited him," said Mr. Findeison. Turning to Max, he added, "Quite a kid I have here."

As Seth sat down on the cushioned chair, he heard tiny voices behind the closed kitchen door, where his mother had corralled the Five Little Monsters.

"I came to thank you, Seth, for what you did," said Max.

"It wasn't anything," said Seth.

"It was, and you know it."

"A lot happened while you were in school," said his father. "Van Arkle left an hour ago."

"What did he find?" asked Seth, although he knew it was good news from their faces and from the fact that his father had let Max in the house.

"It turns out that Gertrude Prescott's story about being in New York the morning of the accident didn't hold water," said Mr. Findeison. "The airline had a record of her on a flight from Philadelphia that afternoon. She missed her first plane and had to take the next one."

"And with Weber's help, they tracked down the body shop in Wilmington," added Max. "With Weber and Mrs. Prescott accusing each other, it looks like I'm not a suspect anymore."

"Then they dropped the charges against you?" Seth asked.

Max nodded. "There are still some details to work out because of the results of the blood test. But my lawyer thinks he can convince them that I did the drinking after I got out of the car."

"Things will work out for the best, I'm sure," said Mr. Findeison.

"I think so." Max put down his cup. "This whole thing gave me a good scare. I know it's time I got help for my drinking problem."

"Hey, Seth. Tell him about tryouts," said his father. "He made first cut, Max."

"How's the competition look?" asked Max.

Seth bit his lip, trying to come up with the response that would satisfy them. "There's a lot of good guys."

"And you'll be right up there with them, too," said Max. He stood up. "Well, I don't want to wear out my welcome."

"I'm glad you came by," Seth said, pleased to see his former coach in high spirits again.

"I know it's not much compared to what you did for me," said Max, "but any time you'd like some extra coaching—you know, some helpful pointers—I'd be more than happy to offer my services."

"Thanks. I'll take you up on that."

"You have a fine young man here," said Max, patting Seth's back.

Mr. Findeison smiled at Seth. "We're very proud of him."

When he saw the pleased expression on his father's face, Seth could no longer bear the gnawing inside him. The moment had come. Yet now that it was time, Seth found that admitting the lie to his dad took more courage than facing Owen Weber.

The Five Little Monsters charged into the living room like wild animals released from a cage. "Can I talk to you upstairs, Dad?" asked Seth.

"Sure. What is it?" Mr Findeison said. He was still smiling. Not for long, thought Seth.

They went up to his parents' bedroom. Mr. Findeison sat on the desk chair. "So talk," he said, pointing to the foot of the bed.

Seth pushed aside the folded afghan his mother had knit the previous winter and sat on the corner of the mattress, facing his father. He didn't want to look at

131

him, but he knew he had to. It was no good unless he said it eye-to-eye.

"Remember that 76ers game we went to last spring, the playoff?" he began. "You know how I really wanted to go? How excited I was when Lee came up with the tickets and asked if I could get you to drive?"

"Sure. Lee's dad had to go out of town, and Jon got the chicken pox, wasn't that it? I drove you guys down to the city. It was a great game."

"I don't remember any of it," said Seth somberly. "Not a single basket."

His father frowned. "I don't get it."

"I did something terrible because of that game." Although he felt as if he were choking on the words, he forced himself to continue. "The night before the game, your supervisor from the mill called. You were outside, so I took the message.

"He said they needed a bunch of guys to work an extra shift the next night, and he called you first." Seth swallowed, trying to push down the lump rising in his throat. "He said he was doing you a favor. He knew the personnel office was making up a new layoff list, and if you came in on short notice, it would show you were behind the company. He said to be sure to tell you that part. You were supposed to call him right away if you wanted the shift.

"When you came inside, you asked me who the phone call was for. Remember, Dad?"

"Go on."

"And I said, 'It was for Hilary, who else?' I didn't give you the message. I knew if you took the shift, you couldn't drive us to the game.

132

"I felt bad about lying, but I thought all it meant was some extra pay. Then the next week, you lost your job. I remembered what the supervisor had said about the layoff list." His eyes filled with tears.

His father stared at him. The proud expression he'd had earlier was gone, replaced by . . . what? Seth wasn't sure.

"Oh son," Mr. Findeison murmured. "Have you been carrying that around with you all this time?"

Nodding, Seth wiped his eyes.

"You should have told me before."

"I know. You could have saved your job."

"That's not what I meant." His father leaned forward, resting his arms on his knees. "You listen to me, Seth. What you did was wrong. If I'd taken that shift I might not have been fired when I was. But nothing could have saved my job. I got tangled up in that union business, and management didn't want a union. I would've lost the job sooner or later." He shook his head. "If you had come to me, I'd have told you that months ago."

"I'm sorry anyway."

"It's over." Mr. Findeison slapped Seth's knee. "Forget it."

"It's not over, Dad. Not the way you've changed. I . . . I hate seeing you sitting around all day unhappy."

Mr. Findeison shrugged. "The only thing I knew was how to work in that mill. I found out there wasn't much else I could do."

"Couldn't you learn to do something else? They

133

have retraining programs, don't they, for plumbers or electricians or some trade like that?''

"Now you sound like your mother."

"Dad, you can't go on like this forever."

His father sighed. "No, I guess I can't. At least I don't want to."

"Will you find out about one of those programs?"

"Okay."

"When?" He wouldn't let his father off the hook.

"Soon."

"Tomorrow?"

His father smiled. "All right. Tomorrow."

Later that evening, Seth rolled up the top of his desk and took out his watercolors and some sheets of paper. He felt better than he had since spring. For several hours he painted. It was the best work he'd ever done. A white seagull, wings extended, flew high above white-capped waves, gliding on gentle air currents. In the background, a patch of blue sky broke through the dark clouds, signaling the end of a storm.

Seth held the watercolor above his desk. That's where it belonged, he decided. He would always keep the painting there to remind him that, like the gull, he could survive a squall and soar again.

What's taking her so long? he thought, as he leaned against the flagpole in front of the junior high building Monday afternoon.

"Seth!"

He looked around and saw Bryan jogging across the grass.

"I've been trying to find you all day. Why weren't you in study hall?"

"I had some work to catch up on in the library," replied Seth.

"It's great news about Max. I saw the article in the newspaper. You're a real hero." He thumped Seth on the back.

Seth brushed Bryan's hand off.

"Come on. You never used to hold grudges."

"I never needed to."

"We're still friends, right?"

"I've got to go. I'm meeting Phoebe Nichol."

"We are, aren't we?" repeated Bryan.

Seth turned his back and walked away. Partway across the lawn, he glanced over his shoulder at Bryan and called, "See you at tryouts later." He knew he wouldn't be ashamed of himself when he left the court that night.

When she saw him waving, Phoebe ran toward him. "I thought you had basketball. You didn't get cut, did you?"

"No. Practice is at 6:00 today." He led her through the crowd to the sidewalk. "I seem to remember that I owe you a Whiz Bang."

"Don't think for a minute that I forgot."

"I was sure you wouldn't." He smiled. "But first, let's go to my house. I have a surprise for you."

"Good, I like surprises," Phoebe said, rubbing her palms together.

They pushed their way through the group waiting for the buses and walked up Beech Street.

"Captain Van Arkle came by yesterday," said Seth,

135

as they crossed at the corner. "The mystery witness finally came forward."

"Who was it?"

"Some lady who lives on Chestnut Street. She didn't want to get involved before. But after reading about Weber and Mrs. Prescott, she changed her mind. Even though she didn't actually see the accident, she saw the Mercedes driving away and says that Mrs. Prescott was at the wheel."

"That's great."

"The great part is that Van Arkle said Mrs. Prescott and her lawyer are working out some deal with the district attorney," said Seth. "I guess she knows she's caught."

"Does that mean that Mrs. Prescott will pay for Hilary's surgery?" asked Phoebe.

"Either her or her insurance company. My parents are taking Hilary to see a plastic surgeon this week."

When they arrived at his house, Seth paused at the front door. "Watch out for the redhead. He kicks."

"One of those? I'll be careful."

"Sethie's got a girlfriend," chanted the Sneak, as soon as Seth opened the door.

"You're just mad because she's not with you," Seth replied, stepping over the Whiner.

Mrs. Findeison came out of the kitchen. "Phoebe, it's good to see you."

"How are you, Mrs. Findeison?"

"Much better these days."

"Don't even think about it, Shin-kicker." Seth grabbed the boy's shoulders as he took aim at Phoebe's leg.

"Maybe you two better run for safety before it's too late," said Mrs. Findeison, taking Shin-kicker's hand. "Try not to wake Hilary."

Stepping lightly, they went upstairs. "Dad put a deadlock on my door after the monsters wrecked the desk," whispered Seth, as he turned the key. "It was the only way to keep them out."

Phoebe followed him into his room and sat down at his desk while he closed the door. "They really trashed it, didn't they?"

"I can fix it," he said.

"It's a fantastic desk, isn't it?"

"I told your aunt about finding it, and she showed me Chandler Prescott's picture. It was funny the way she talked about him. I wonder if there was something between them once."

Phoebe smiled. "I didn't know you were so romantic."

He raised an eyebrow. "You don't know *everything* about me, Phoebe, believe it or not."

She laughed. "Hey, this is new," she said, noticing the watercolor over his desk. "The seagull looks so real."

He reached for a sheet of paper on top of his dresser. "I hope you like this one, too. It's your surprise. Kind of a thank you."

"For what?"

"For helping me. For being a good friend."

She took the watercolor from his hand. "What a beautiful sunset!"

He waited to see if she noticed the rest.

After a few moments, she looked up from the pa-

137

per. "This tree in the corner, at the top of the hill—it's our tree house tree, isn't it?"

He nodded.

"And somewhere near the top, hidden behind the orange and red leaves, you and I are sitting, waiting for the stars to come out. I like to think of us that way."

"Me, too," he said.

Suddenly, he heard a shuffling sound at the door.

"We're being spied on," Seth whispered, as he tiptoed across the room.

He yanked open the door, and two pairs of startled eyes stared at him from the floor. Seth growled like a bogeyman, and in a flash, the Sneak and the Human Wrecking Ball were on their feet, racing down the hall.

Phoebe giggled. "I think you'd better soundproof your door and plug up your keyhole, too."

"Maybe I'll have to move to the garage." He sighed as he closed the door.

Alone in the room again, Seth and Phoebe stared at each other in awkward silence. What happens next? Seth wondered. How would things be between them from then on?

Phoebe reached over and punched his arm. "Hey, you owe me a Whiz Bang. Are you going to pay up or not?"

Smiling, Seth lightly returned the punch. Things between them were going to be just fine. "Come on," he said. "I'll race you."